"I'm not sure what kind of coven I want to join, actually," Kate answered Annie. "I guess I hadn't thought too much about it. I'll have to wait to hear what the other presenters have to say."

"Sure," Annie remarked.

She snuck a glance at Kate. Her friend hadn't asked her what *she* was looking for in a coven. Did Kate care whether or not they were in the same one? Was it important to her to continue working with Annie? Annie realized that she was basing her decision, at least in part, on what Kate wanted to do. But was that the right thing? Annie had assumed that with Cooper gone she and Kate would want to stick together. But maybe she'd been wrong. Suddenly the little circle of three that she, Kate, and Cooper had made seemed to be falling apart, and that scared her more than she wanted to admit.

Follow the Circle:

circle of three

BOOK
15

initiation

isobel bird

AVON BOOKS

An Imprint of HarperCollinsPublishers

Initiation

Copyright © 2002 by Isobel Bird

Printed in the United States of America.
For information address HarperCollins Children's Books,
a division of HarperCollins Publishers,
1350 Avenue of the Americas,
New York, NY 10019.

Library of Congress Catalog Card Number: 2001118055
ISBN 0-06-000607-2

First Avon edition, 2002

❖

AVON TRADEMARK REG. U.S. PAT. OFF. AND IN OTHER COUNTRIES,
MARCA REGISTRADA, HECHO EN U.S.A.

Visit us on the World Wide Web!
www.harperteen.com

CHAPTER I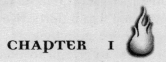

"Do you think maybe you've had enough of those?"
Jane asked Cooper.

"No," Cooper said defensively. "I don't."

"Well, at least slow down," her friend told her.
"If you keep downing them at that rate you're going
to be sick, and that would *not* be pretty."

"Don't worry," replied Cooper. "I can hold my
Oreos."

She took another cookie from the box and
dunked it into the glass of milk she was holding. She
let the cookie get good and wet, then popped it into
her mouth and chewed. Jane watched her, a look of
concern on her face.

"Do you really think eating Oreos is the answer
to this?" she asked Cooper.

"Probably not," Cooper responded, her mouth
full. "But it can't hurt."

"I don't know about that," remarked Jane. "I
think you're on a sugar high. When you crash,

it's going to be nasty."

"Who says I'm going to crash?" Cooper said. "I'm just going to keep eating these things one after the other. That way I'll never come down."

"And you'll gain thirty-five pounds," said Jane, giving Cooper a stern look.

"I refuse to give in to ridiculous standards of female beauty," Cooper said. "Big is beautiful."

She picked up another cookie, started to put it in her mouth, and then put it down. She set the glass of milk on the table and sighed.

"Fine," she said. "So maybe stuffing myself with crispy chocolate and creamy white filling goodness isn't exactly the most productive way to deal with this."

"That's better," Jane said, pushing the box of Oreos out of Cooper's reach. "Now, do you want to talk or not?"

Cooper slumped in her chair. "I just hate thinking about Kate and Annie being at initiation class while I'm here," she said unhappily.

Jane was quiet for a minute. "Can you maybe talk to Sophia?" she asked.

"I *did* that," answered Cooper. "All she said was that they didn't think I was quite ready." She paused a moment. "I don't get it," she continued. "I completed my challenge. I faced my greatest fear. So why don't they think I'm ready? I mean, of everyone there I probably have the most experience with Wicca in the first place. Plus, I've done a lot during the past year. I helped a dead girl find her murderer. I was hazed by faeries. I made Beecher Falls High School safe for pentacle-wearing pagans everywhere. Oh, and I helped stop a totally insane ghost from turning us all into icicles."

She looked at Jane as if she expected a response, but before the other girl could say anything Cooper started ranting again. "That doesn't even include the fact that I got a boyfriend, quit one band and started another one, survived my parents' getting divorced and my mother's temporary drinking issues, had my name all over the papers not once but twice, and started jogging."

"Are you done now?" asked Jane when Cooper stopped talking.

Cooper nodded.

"All those things are great," Jane said. "If you were applying to witch college, I'm sure they'd be very impressed by your extracurricular activities and give you a full scholarship."

"Hey!" Cooper said, sounding hurt.

"Let me finish," Jane told her. "What I was going to say is that maybe you can't look at this that way. Being invited to be initiated wasn't a competition. It was an individual thing. Just because you started out ahead of most people doesn't necessarily mean you learned as much as they did. Maybe they just felt that you hadn't quite done everything you were supposed to."

"Thank you," Cooper said when Jane was done

speaking. "I feel so much better now I can't tell you. Not only do I feel like a loser for not making it to initiation, I also feel like a self-absorbed jerk who thinks she's better than her friends. Give me back those cookies."

Jane swatted Cooper's hand away as she reached for the Oreos. Then she took the cookies and dumped them into the garbage can beside the sink. When Cooper glared at her, Jane said, "I'm saving you from yourself. You'll thank me later."

"Who says I won't just fish them out of there?" Cooper replied angrily.

"Go right ahead," Jane told her. "I hope you like your Oreos mixed with old coffee grinds and potato peelings, because that's what they're covered in now."

"I don't know why I asked you to come over," said Cooper huffily.

"Because you knew no one else would put up with you when you're in this kind of mood," Jane replied, leaning against the counter and folding her arms across her chest. "T.J. is probably hiding in his room, afraid to answer the phone. Plus, you knew that I still owed you one for the time you came to see me in the hospital after my little mock suicide attempt." She gave Cooper a sad face, blinking her eyes and pouting her lips.

"You are so tragically gay," Cooper told Jane, and the two of them erupted in laughter. When they stopped, Cooper stood up. "Let's go play some music," she said.

The two girls went upstairs to Cooper's room, where they got out their guitars. Jane settled into Cooper's desk chair, while Cooper sat on the edge of the bed. Jane began to play something, and Cooper joined in. It was a song they'd been fooling around with for a couple of weeks, something that had emerged from one of their writing sessions. But it hadn't quite come together yet.

"This might not be the best time to bring this up," Jane said as they played. "But how would you feel about doing a gig?"

"What kind of gig?" Cooper asked tentatively.

"I was at the Record Vault the other day," Jane said. "Looking for some Divinyls discs. You know, the old ones with the punk stuff on them where Christina really wails. Anyway, I saw this flyer. One of the clubs is having a women in rock night, and it's looking for bands."

Cooper groaned. "Women in rock?" she said.

"I know," Jane replied. "It's kind of our worst nightmare. But I don't think this is all Lilith Fair or anything. It sounds more hard-core. Betty Bangs is one of the judges."

"Betty Bangs?" Cooper said, suddenly sounding interested. "As in Betty Bangs from Scrapple?"

"The very same," said Jane.

Cooper continued to play while she thought about it. "I don't know," she said. "What would we play?"

"I thought we could do some of the new stuff

we've been working on," Jane answered. "The show is on the thirty-first."

"That's like a week and a half!" said Cooper.

"I know," Jane said. "It's okay. Forget about it. I just thought it might be fun."

"No," Cooper said. "It *would* be fun. Let's do it."

"You're sure?" Jane asked.

Cooper nodded. "Yeah," she said. "We can be ready with the new stuff by then."

Jane smiled. "Good thing I signed us up, then," she said. "The bill is probably full by now."

Cooper threw her guitar pick at Jane. "Just for that I'm making you wear an O-Town T-shirt the night of the show," she said.

They played for an hour or so, trying out different things. Then it was time for Jane to leave. After Cooper walked her friend to the door, she returned to her room and picked up her guitar again. She played around on it for a minute, then set it down. Despite the enthusiasm she'd displayed for her friend, she really wasn't in the mood for music at all.

In fact, she wasn't really in the mood for much besides feeling sorry for herself. She'd hoped that asking Jane to come over would distract her, and it had, but only for a moment. Now that Jane was gone, the dark depression that had been following Cooper around returned. It had been there ever since the previous Tuesday, when she'd learned that she wouldn't be getting initiated into Wicca along with her friends. Thinking about seeing the candle that signified the decision of the class teachers refuse to light when she'd held her match to it, Cooper once again felt the agonizing pain she'd felt that night as she'd realized that she'd failed.

She also felt confused. She honestly didn't know how she could have possibly failed. She'd done everything right. Or at least she'd thought that she had. Although she didn't want to, she couldn't help but compare her performance to the performances of Kate and Annie during the year that they'd been studying Wicca together. Had they really done that much better than she had? She couldn't see how. In fact, if she had to rate her friends she would have to say that she was probably better than they were at some things. Plus, she had never badly messed up a spell, like Kate had, or caused any trouble by trying to aspect a goddess, like Annie had. All of *her* spells had pretty much worked out the way they were supposed to.

So then why are Annie and Kate over at Crones' Circle while you're sitting here? she asked herself.

"That's a good question," she said out loud.

She looked at the clock. It was almost nine. She knew that class would probably be just about over. Should she call Kate or Annie and ask what they'd done? Part of her really wanted to know. But it would be too humiliating to ask them. She'd feel like someone who hadn't been invited to a party asking for details about the food and what had gone on from someone who had been there. She couldn't do that. It had been difficult enough just talking to her friends after the embarrassment of not being chosen for initiation. None of them really discussed it, and she knew that Kate and Annie were careful not to say too much about Wicca when she was around. That only made things worse, but Cooper wasn't sure how to fix that. If they *did* talk about it, she would only get upset because she would feel left out. But when they didn't talk about it, it made her feel like she was preventing them from talking about something important.

Things couldn't go on like that. She knew that. Kate and Annie were going to be initiated. She didn't expect them to refuse to go through with it just because she hadn't been chosen. And she herself was still very much into witchcraft. After all, even Sophia and Archer had said that just because they weren't being asked to participate in initiation they shouldn't stop studying Wicca and practicing magic. Cooper fully intended to keep doing exactly that. It was a part of her life, and she wasn't going to give it up.

But that didn't mean it didn't hurt her to think about not being with her two friends when they were made full-fledged witches. They'd all talked about how cool it would be finally being members of a working coven. They'd all assumed that they would be together or, even if they chose to be in different covens, at least they would all be witches together. But now things had changed. Now Annie and Kate would be witches while Cooper would just be someone who studied Wicca.

Maybe you can do the year and a day over again, she told herself. After all, she knew that Sasha planned on doing the dedication ceremony and beginning her journey down the Wiccan path. Jane had been talking about maybe doing it, too. Perhaps Cooper could join them. *But that would feel like being sent to remedial ed or something*, she thought bitterly. *Summer school for witches.*

And what if she was denied initiation again after that? That would be way too much to bear. What if there was just some fundamental personality flaw in her that made Sophia and the others think she would be a really bad witch? Her conversation with Sophia had been difficult. Cooper had been reluctant to talk to her, but she'd forced herself to do it. Sophia had been very kind, saying that she and the other teachers simply felt that Cooper wasn't quite ready for initiation yet. She hadn't given Cooper any specific reasons, and Cooper had been too embarrassed to ask for any. As a result, she'd spent the past few days coming up with reasons of her own, a pastime that made her even more miserable.

When the phone rang Cooper jumped. She looked at it for a moment, hesitating before picking it up. "Hello?" she said warily, afraid it might be

Kate or Annie wanting to talk about class.

"You've got to save me." It was T.J. He sounded slightly hysterical.

"Why?" Cooper asked him, thoughts about herself pushed from her mind as she worried that he might be in trouble. "What's wrong?"

"Our mothers are driving me crazy," T.J. replied.

Cooper grinned despite herself. Her mother and Mrs. McAllister had been spending a lot of time together in recent weeks. That night they had gone to dinner. Apparently they had ended up at the McAllisters' house afterward.

"What are they doing?" Cooper asked her boyfriend.

"At the moment they're looking at photo albums," T.J. answered. "Your mother seems particularly amused by the pictures my mother took of me dressed as a pink bunny rabbit for Halloween when I was four."

"I can see why," remarked Cooper. "I wouldn't mind getting a look at those myself."

"Ha ha," T.J. said. "Anyway, I just wanted to call and see how you are."

"I'm okay," said Cooper. "Jane just left. We worked on some stuff."

"Okay," T.J. said. "Now tell me the truth. How are you?"

"I ate a box of Oreos," admitted Cooper. "Well, not a whole box. Jane took them away from me."

"Smart move," said T.J. "Can I do anything to cheer you up?"

"Hold that thought," Cooper said. "Someone is beeping in."

She put T.J. on hold and answered the second call. "Hello?"

"Hi, honey," said her father.

"Hey there," said Cooper. "Hang on. I have to say good-bye to T.J."

This time she put her father on hold while she switched back to her boyfriend. "I have to go," she said.

"A better offer?" T.J. asked.

"My dad," Cooper told him. "I haven't talked to him in a while because he was out of town. Should I call you back?"

"No," T.J. said. "I'm going to go out to the garage to play for a while before Mom starts showing your mother photos of me in the bathtub."

"Ooh," Cooper said. "That could be embarrassing."

"Tell me about it," said T.J. "Especially since I was fifteen when she took them."

"Very funny," replied Cooper, laughing at his joke. "Tell her not to stay up too late. And thanks for calling. That does make me feel better." She lied. *It won't do anyone any good to make him feel bad, too,* she thought.

T.J. hung up, and Cooper switched back to her dad. "Sorry about that," she said.

"No problem," Mr. Rivers said. "I always knew I'd lose you to a boy sometime. If it has to happen, I'm glad it's T.J."

"Please," Cooper said. "Don't start tossing rice just yet."

"So, how are things?" her father asked her.

"Okay," Cooper answered. "Mom is fine. I'm fine. We're fine."

"Hmm," Mr. Rivers said. "All of those fines sound awfully suspicious."

"No," Cooper said. "Really. Everything is pretty much fine. How about you?" she asked, changing the subject.

"Oh, fine," said Mr. Rivers.

It was Cooper's turn to be suspicious. "That fine didn't sound so fine," she said. "What's up?"

"Well," said her father, "there *is* something I want to talk to you about."

"I told you, I really am thinking about colleges," said Cooper, not wanting to get into that particular annoying discussion.

"It's not about college," Mr. Rivers said. "It's about me. I'm sort of seeing somebody."

Cooper was taken aback by her father's statement. "Seeing someone?" she said. "I take it you mean as in seeing a shrink, or seeing a proctologist, right?"

"No," Mr. Rivers answered. "I mean as in I'm dating someone."

"Dating?" said Cooper. "But the divorce was

only, like, ten minutes ago."

"The paperwork might have been completed recently, but the emotional separation happened a long time ago, Cooper," her father said. "Look, I know this is hard to hear. But I wanted you to know so that when you meet this woman it won't be so awkward."

"Meet her," Cooper parroted. *He wants me to meet her?* she thought.

Her father sounded excited. Cooper wanted to be happy for him, but she was still having trouble accepting that he was dating someone. She listened to him talk, but heard almost nothing of what he said until he asked, "So dinner on Friday is okay with you?"

"What?" Cooper said.

"Dinner," her father repeated. "On Friday. The three of us."

"Oh, sure," Cooper said without thinking. "That would be fine."

"Good," Mr. Rivers said. "How about seven o'clock at Shiva's Garden?"

"Okay," said Cooper. Shiva's Garden was a cool vegetarian Indian restaurant. Cooper loved it, but she knew it wasn't her father's favorite. If they were having dinner there he *really* wanted her to like this woman.

She hung up and flung herself backward on the bed. Suddenly it seemed as if every aspect of her life had been thrown off course. Everything had been going along pretty well for a while. Her mother was doing okay. She and T.J. were happy. She'd been looking forward to the end of her year and a day of studying Wicca. Now she wasn't being initiated, it looked like she and T.J. would be going to different colleges after they graduated, and her father was dating someone. What else could possibly happen?

"Don't ask that," she scolded herself as she closed her eyes and tried not to think about what her mother would say when she heard that Cooper's father was dating someone—as she eventually would. "You probably don't want to know."

CHAPTER 2

"I know a lot of you are looking at your upcoming initiation as the end of a long journey," Sophia said to the seven people seated in the back room of Crones' Circle. "You've all worked very hard for the past year, and now the final destination is in sight, right?"

The three men and four women all laughed and nodded.

Sophia smiled. "Well, you're wrong," she said. "This isn't the end; it's the beginning. It's the beginning of a lifetime of learning and exploring and discovering. Why do you think they call your graduation from high school a commencement service? Because it's the beginning of the rest of your life, the start of the journey you were *really* preparing for when you suffered through algebra and gym class."

There was more laughter from the class members in response to Sophia's comment. Annie and Kate, the only two members of the class still in high school, looked at one another knowingly.

"Your initiation is really a commencement," Sophia continued. "Your year and a day of study taught you a great deal about yourselves—about your abilities and your weaknesses. You've come to know yourselves better, and you've come to understand Wicca better. But you're still just beginning. I was initiated more than twenty-five years ago, and I still don't know all there is to know about Wicca, or about myself." She paused, looking thoughtful, and then added, "I think probably there are some things about myself I *don't* want to know."

Annie listened as Sophia continued her speech. It was the first of four preparatory classes before the initiation ceremony itself. When they'd begun their year and a day, the thought of initiation had been a distant one. Annie hadn't really even allowed herself to think a lot about the actual event itself because it had seemed so far off. But now that it was just about there, four weeks seemed almost too short a time to prepare. Suddenly, Annie could only think about everything she *didn't* know about witchcraft. It was the same feeling she sometimes got before a big test, like she had forgotten to study something really important and would be asked to write an essay about the topic, or she'd learned the wrong list of events or formulas and would have no idea how to work out the problems.

Relax, she told herself. *You made it this far.* She looked around at the other six people who had been selected for initiation. Of the nearly twenty people who had started the class, the seven of them were all that remained. Several people had dropped out during the course of the year, either because they couldn't find the time for the class or because they'd decided they weren't really interested in Wicca enough to devote that kind of energy to it. Several more had made it to the end but decided that they didn't want to undergo formal initiation. And still others had not been offered initiation.

Like Cooper, Annie thought sadly. She still couldn't believe that Cooper had been one of the people whose candle hadn't lit during the choosing ceremony. She still recalled the look of pain, anger, and sadness she'd seen on her friend's face as Cooper had rushed from the store that night. Annie and Kate had gone after her, but Cooper had been determined to get away from them. Kate had wanted to keep chasing her, but Annie had stopped her, knowing that Cooper wasn't angry at them but just wanted to be alone for a while.

Although the three of them had talked only briefly about Cooper's failure, Annie and Kate had talked about it extensively in private. Neither of them could figure out what had happened. Annie had even tried to bring the subject up with Archer once, but Archer had kindly but firmly informed Annie that the decision was a private matter between the dedicant and the teachers, and refused to say anything else. Since then the subject had become one that no one mentioned in front of Cooper, although it was always there, waiting for one of them to trip over.

And it's only going to get worse, Annie thought sadly. The fact was, she, Cooper, and Kate were best friends. There was no way Annie and Kate could immerse themselves in Wicca the way they would be doing after initiation and not be able to talk about it around Cooper. That just couldn't happen, which meant one of two things: either Cooper was going to have to deal with not being initiated with them or . . . She couldn't allow herself to think about the other option. But try as she might, she had to. *Or the three of us won't be able to be best friends anymore*, she told herself.

That, however, was a possibility she couldn't even imagine. Not be best friends with Cooper? *Well, you barely knew who she was a year ago*, she argued with herself. That was true. The first time Annie had even spoken to Cooper was after Kate had enlisted Annie's help to correct the effects of a botched spell and the two of them had in turn had to ask Cooper for assistance. Thinking about the moment when she had confronted a reluctant Cooper in one of the school's music rehearsal rooms, Annie couldn't help but smile. She'd been so intimidated by the tough-acting Cooper, with her sarcastic responses and her cool demeanor. It had taken a lot for Annie to stand up to her and break through Cooper's wall of reserve. But she had, and she had quickly come to appreciate Cooper's unique personality. Thinking that maybe she wouldn't be spending as much time with her friend saddened her.

"We won't be discussing any details of the initiation ceremony itself," Sophia said, bringing Annie's attention back to the subject at hand. "But don't worry, there won't be any last-minute make-or-break questions or weird challenges or anything. This isn't some TV reality show, where we make you vote one another out or eat sheep eyes or anything like that."

"Darn, and I've been practicing with the sheep eyes," said Ben, one of the three men undergoing initiation.

"Well, we can always add them especially for you," remarked Sophia. "But I think probably we'll have better things to eat than that. Now, the real purpose of these last four classes is to get you to think about covens. As you all know by now, many—but not all—witches work within covens. You've seen several covens in action, at least during public rituals, and you have some idea of how things differ from coven to coven. Every coven has its own way of doing things, from casting circles to working magic to celebrating the sabbats. It's important that you align yourself with a coven that you think will both be a comfortable place for you to work and also challenge you to grow in your own practice of witchcraft."

"You mean we're going to get choices?" asked Emma, one of the four female initiates.

Sophia nodded. "As you've probably guessed by now, we don't exactly always do things by the book around here," she said, suppressing a grin. "Traditionally you would all be trained by one particular coven for your year and a day of study, after which you would then be asked to join that coven. Not here. Here we take a different approach. During the past year you've received teaching from a number of different people from a number of different covens. You've also attended sabbat rituals involving participants from many different covens. That's because we wanted you to experience a wide range of the ways in which Wicca is practiced. Our initiation process will be conducted in much the same way, but with a twist."

Annie looked at Kate. "What kind of twist?" she whispered.

"Good question," said Sophia, hearing her and making Annie blush. "The twist is that you probably won't all undergo the same initiation ceremony."

Again, Annie and Kate looked at one another in confusion.

"We'll use our remaining classes to explore the different types of covens in more depth," Sophia explained. "You will then each choose the coven you think is most appropriate for you. If the leaders of that coven agree, you will then be initiated into that coven. Because each coven has its own way of performing initiations, that part will not be done together."

"And what if they don't want you?" queried Ezra, a quiet man in his late thirties who had been one of the choices for initiation that had sort of surprised Annie. Ezra had rarely contributed to class discussions, and he was one of the people Annie knew the least about. But now he was one of the final seven. The other six turned to regard him.

"I just ask because I've sort of been through this kind of thing before," Ezra said, clearly nervous about being paid attention to. "I'm a doctor, and when you do your final residency you have to list your first, second, and third choices for hospitals to work at. Everyone in the country finds out on the same day which choice they got, and it can be really horrible if you don't match up with one of your choices."

"Don't worry," Sophia told him. "This isn't quite the same thing. It's very informal. Very seldom do people ask for covens that aren't right for them. In general we find that it's one of those mystical experiences where everything works out pretty much the way it should. But try not to worry about that. Just sit back and listen to what the different coven leaders have to say."

Annie leaned back and tried to relax. She saw Kate doing the same thing, and she wondered what her friend was thinking about. Annie was thinking about whether or not they would choose the same coven. She'd always assumed that they would end up together. *But maybe we won't,* she thought. *After all, you also thought Cooper would be here, and she isn't.* Once again Annie was struck by how you could never count on things' going in a particular way. Time and again the truth of that had been revealed to her through her magical work.

Look at Aunt Sarah and Mr. Dunning, she reminded herself. She would never in a million years have guessed that her aunt would be marrying the author of one of Annie's favorite book series, or that they would have met because that author was living in the house where Annie had grown up. But he did live there, and her aunt *was* marrying him—only a few days before Annie's initiation. That was a whole other thing to think about, but Annie would have to do it later. Right now it was time to pay attention to learning about covens.

"Since you've spent a great deal of the past year looking at my face," Sophia said, "I might as well tell you something about the coven *I'm* a part of."

Annie quickly forgot about the other questions and concerns on her mind. She knew that Sophia was part of the coven that owned and ran Crones' Circle. However, Sophia had never been particularly clear about exactly what that coven did. Annie didn't even know its name.

"A lot of you probably think we've been very mysterious about our coven," said Sophia, voicing Annie's thoughts. "Let me assure you that we weren't trying to hide anything from you. We just wanted you to be open to all the different types of teaching and practicing that you've experienced. Sometimes when students know too much about a teacher's particular background it makes it difficult for them to be as open to other possibilities. We try to avoid that in our class by not saying too much about our own coven. Until now, that is."

Sophia held up a black three-ring binder. "This is the Book of Shadows for the Daughters of the Cauldron, which is the name of my coven."

Annie looked at the Book of Shadows in Sophia's hand. She knew a Book of Shadows was the collection of a coven's—or an individual witch's—rituals and everything pertaining to them. It might include attempted spells and their outcomes, lyrics to chants and songs, accounts of how various sabbats were celebrated, ideas for future rituals, initiation instructions, and basically anything else of importance to the coven. It was, really, a journal of the coven's life and work, and its contents were generally closely guarded, revealed only to people within the coven. Annie herself kept a personal Book of Shadows, a notebook in which she recorded the different spells and rituals she tried and where she wrote her thoughts about Wicca and its role in her life.

Sophia waved the Book of Shadows in the air. "As you can see, this looks sort of like a cookbook," she remarked as some loose pages fluttered out and fell to the ground. "That's because that's sort of how we see it. The members of the Daughters of the Cauldron are what are sometimes termed kitchen witches. That means that we don't really have a formal way of doing things. We take a little of this and a little of that and add it together to see what happens. Sometimes what we come up with tastes great. And sometimes, as anyone who has ever cooked will tell you, what we come up with isn't the tastiest thing ever created."

Annie, who did a lot of cooking, laughed. Kitchen witches. She liked the sound of that. It reminded her of working on a recipe, deciding what to put in and what to leave out, stirring everything and then tasting it. She also liked the name of Sophia's coven—the Daughters of the Cauldron.

"The Daughters of the Cauldron was formed about twenty years ago," Sophia continued. "It was started by me and my friend Tove. We also started this bookstore together, to give people interested in Wicca a place to study. It started out as more of a community center with a few books, and over the years it's gone through a lot of changes. But it has always been run by our coven. Tove died several years ago, but I think she still stops in to visit from time to time," Sophia added, smiling wistfully.

"What do you mean when you say your coven isn't as formal as others?" asked Laura, who sat beside Annie.

"I mean we don't have a formal structure, as some covens do," Sophia explained. "We don't have one single person who leads. We take turns. Members are encouraged to come up with ideas for rituals, and we let people use their imaginations when casting our circles and that sort of thing. We also don't draw from any one single tradition. We feel comfortable mixing aspects of Greek mythology with Celtic, for example, or using the name of a Japanese goddess and a Norse god in ritual. Like I said, when we get together it's like a bunch of cooks standing around the same stove."

"Well, with three kids and a husband to cook for every day, I can relate," Laura said, laughing.

"That's something else I should mention," said Sophia. "While we don't exclude men from our coven, we generally have been mostly women. I don't know why, exactly, but that's the way it's worked out. So if any of you guys want to join, keep in mind that you'll be really outnumbered."

"How many are there in your coven?" asked Roger, a college student who was the last of the three men being initiated.

"Right now there are a dozen or so," said Sophia. "Sometimes I lose count. Again, not to discourage anyone, but we don't want to add too many more, so hopefully you won't all decide that you simply *have* to be Daughters of the Cauldron."

"Or sons," Ben remarked.

"Or sons," agreed Sophia. "But we aren't changing the name, so keep that in mind."

"What's the group's primary focus?" asked Emma.

"When we formed the coven, Tove and I believed that magic should be about working for change," Sophia answered. "We wanted the Daughters of the Cauldron to focus on using magic to create change in ourselves and in the world. That's why this store is a cooperative. Our members are also encouraged to do volunteer work and to find unique ways of expressing their interest in witchcraft in other aspects of their lives. Apart from that, we're a very unfocused bunch."

Sophia looked around. "Okay," she said. "If there aren't any questions, that's going to be it for tonight. Next time we'll hear from two other covens, one of which you all know pretty well and the other of which will be mostly new to you. If any of you want to stay and ask me more questions about my coven, I'll be happy to answer them. Otherwise, we'll see you next week. Try to use the time between now and then to really think about what you want from your coven. That will make it easier to start narrowing your choices down."

The class members stood up and began rearranging the room. Annie saw Ben and Laura go up to talk to Sophia, while she helped Kate pile cushions against one of the walls.

"The Daughters of the Cauldron sounds interesting," Annie said as they straightened the pile.

"Yeah," said Kate. "I don't know if it's for me, though. Having my mother run a catering business puts me in contact with enough cooking. I think I'd like my coven to be something different."

Annie felt slightly disappointed hearing Kate say that. She'd sort of been thinking that the Daughters of the Cauldron might be perfect for her. But if Kate didn't want to be in it, she wasn't sure she did either.

"I'm not sure what kind of coven I want, actually," Kate said. "I guess I hadn't thought too much about it. I'll have to wait to hear what the other people have to say."

"Sure," Annie remarked.

She snuck a glance at Kate. Her friend hadn't asked her what *she* was looking for in a coven. Did Kate care whether or not they were in the same one? Was it important to her to continue working with Annie? Annie realized that she was basing her decision, at least in part, on what Kate wanted to do. But was that the right thing? Annie had assumed

that with Cooper gone she and Kate would want to
stick together. But maybe she'd been wrong.
Suddenly the little circle of three that she, Kate, and
Cooper had made seemed to be falling apart, and
that scared her more than she wanted to admit.

CHAPTER 3

When Kate came home from school on Wednesday afternoon, she found her mother sitting in the kitchen with Annie's Aunt Sarah. The two women were drinking coffee, and Sarah Crandall was looking at the menu Mrs. Morgan had proposed for her wedding to Grayson Dunning.

"I had no idea there were so many different kinds of cheese," Annie's aunt said.

"It can be a little overwhelming," Kate's mother replied. "But basically what it comes down to is whether you want soft cheese or hard cheese. Since you're having strawberries, I suggest you go with a soft cheese like Brie."

"Fine," said Aunt Sarah. "Whatever you say."

Mrs. Morgan made a note on the yellow pad in front of her. "I wish all my clients were as easy to please as you are," she commented.

"They probably would be if they were even half as lost and behind schedule as I am," replied Aunt Sarah. "I can't believe we're going to pull this off.

We have less than three weeks, and I still haven't ordered the flowers. I haven't even looked at *dresses*," she added, sounding slightly hysterical.

"It will be fine," Mrs. Morgan told her. "You've almost got the food done, and that's one of the biggest parts."

"I'm just glad it's a small wedding," Aunt Sarah told her. "Anything bigger than this and they'd have to institutionalize me afterward."

"Trust me," said Kate's mother. "I've seen some brides who almost were."

Kate went to the refrigerator and took out a can of soda. "I hear Meg and Annie are going to be bridesmaids," she said.

"Along with Becka," Aunt Sarah said, sighing. "Believe me, getting the three of them to agree on dresses has been one of my biggest headaches. Meg says she doesn't want to look like a little girl. Becka doesn't want to look too frilly. And Annie wants us to go with a Victorian garden look. Now you tell me, how are we supposed to make everyone happy?"

"You can't," Mrs. Morgan said. "So stop worrying about it. What does Grayson say about it all?"

Aunt Sarah sighed. "He's so busy trying to get his next book out and plan for the move that he can't think about anything else," she said. "I think he'd be happy if we just ran off to Vegas instead."

Kate sat down at the table and took a drink of her

soda. "What about a theme wedding?" she asked.

Annie's aunt looked at her curiously. "What kind of theme?" she asked.

Kate thought. "How about *Alice in Wonderland*?" she suggested. "You could be Alice. Mr. Dunning could be the White Rabbit."

"Better make him the Mad Hatter," Aunt Sarah said, playing along.

"Okay," Kate said. "Then Meg could be the White Rabbit, or maybe the Dormouse. Annie could be the Queen of Hearts. Oh, and Becka could be the Cheshire Cat. That would suit her."

Aunt Sarah looked at Mrs. Morgan. "Think you could pull off treacle tarts and a big tea party?" she asked.

"It can't be any harder than the seven hundred crab cakes and eighty gallons of chowder I had to make for the Bean family wedding last year," Kate's mother said.

"I don't know about Annie as the Queen of Hearts, though," said Aunt Sarah. "That seems a little too harsh for her. What other characters were there?"

"Tweedle Dee and Tweedle Dum," Kate said, trying to recall the story.

"The March Hare," added Mrs. Morgan.

"The Caterpillar," said Aunt Sarah, grinning. "That's perfect for her."

"A bug?" Kate said doubtfully. "I don't know."

"No," Aunt Sarah said. "The Caterpillar was very wise and very mysterious. Annie will love it."

"It would be interesting," Kate said, still unsure of the choice of the Caterpillar for her friend.

"I'm sure she'll do it," said Aunt Sarah. "Besides, it would be perfect if Becka is the Cheshire Cat and Meg is the White Rabbit. All three of them helped Alice find what she was looking for."

"What about the guests?" asked Kate.

Aunt Sarah shrugged. "There are only thirty of them," she said. "They can wear whatever they want to. But how fun would it be if the servers were dressed as playing cards?" she asked, looking hopefully at Mrs. Morgan.

"I can try," Kate's mother said. "But I'm not promising."

"Oh, and the minister," said Aunt Sarah. "*She* should be the Queen of Hearts. I know she'd get a big kick out of that." She turned to Kate. "This is the best idea," she said. "Suddenly this feels like a party and not a chore."

"Yes, but now you have to worry about costumes," Mrs. Morgan reminded her.

"Juliet," said Kate suddenly. "Juliet can do it. She's a costume designer, remember?"

Aunt Sarah beamed. "Brilliant!" she said. "I've been looking for a way to include her in the wedding. This is absolutely perfect. I'll call her tonight and see if she can do it."

For the next hour the three of them elaborated on the new wedding theme. Now that they had something to work with, it was easy to keep building on the idea. Mrs. Morgan suggested food that would be perfect for a tea party atmosphere, and Kate made recommendations for decorations.

"It will be too early in the year for roses," she said. "But we can make fake ones out of crepe paper and attach them to the bushes. It will look just like the rose garden where Alice plays croquet."

"I can't wait to tell Grayson about this," Aunt Sarah said, getting ready to leave. "*Alice in Wonderland* was the book that made him want to write when he was a little boy. He'll definitely go for this."

"I hope so," Mrs. Morgan commented as she stood up to show Aunt Sarah to the door. "I'm kind of excited about making these tarts."

Kate waved good-bye to Annie's aunt as she left. When Mrs. Morgan returned she patted Kate on the back. "Good work," she said. "I thought she was going to have a breakdown if I asked her to choose between asparagus puffs and chilled shrimp. You made things a lot easier with that Wonderland idea."

"Thanks," Kate said. "Does that mean I get a commission?"

"No," her mother answered. "But it means you

don't have to carry around trays of shrimp."

"I'll settle for that," replied Kate. "Oh, but if you do need people, I know Tara and Jess would be happy to do it."

"That would be great," her mother said as she tidied up the table. "And I almost forgot. Tyler called for you."

"Tyler?" Kate repeated.

Her mother nodded. Then she gave Kate a questioning look. "Anything I should know?"

Kate shook her head. "If there is, it's something I should know, too," she replied. "I have no idea why he called me."

"Well, he wanted you to call him back," Mrs. Morgan said.

Kate stood up. "Thanks," she said, leaving the kitchen and heading up to her room. When she got there she picked up the phone and looked at it for a moment. It had been so long since she'd called Tyler that she wasn't sure she remembered the number. But after a moment she did, and dialed it as if she'd never forgotten it.

As the phone rang she wondered what Tyler might want. They hadn't spoken since a few months before, when he had asked her to go out with him again and she'd said no. She hadn't even seen him around Crones' Circle very much, and whenever she ran into his mother, Rowan, she was careful not to bring up Tyler's name. It felt a little strange to her, basically pretending that her exboyfriend didn't exist, but it had been the easiest way to deal with things. But now Tyler apparently had something to say to her.

"Hello?"

Kate jumped when she heard Tyler's voice. It sounded strange over the phone, and for a moment she thought she might have dialed the wrong number. But then she realized it was just Tyler with a cold.

"Are you sick?" she asked.

"Hello to you, too," replied Tyler. He sneezed. "Yes, I'm sick," he said. "I caught a cold during our Ostara ritual."

Ostara, the Spring Equinox, had been on Tuesday. Because they'd had class that night, Kate and the others had celebrated the sabbat the previous Saturday. It had been a time of mixed emotions for Kate. She'd been looking forward to it because it marked the anniversary of the first official sabbat that she, Annie, and Cooper had celebrated with other Wiccans. At the Ostara ritual the year before they had met Sophia and the others who had become their teachers. They had also met their friend Sasha. Those were all good memories, and it should have been a happy time.

But several dark clouds had hung over the occasion. The three friends had been asked months before to help organize and run the ritual. They'd spent a lot of time coming up with chants and activities, and they'd been looking forward to seeing all of their hard work pay off. But then Cooper had failed to be chosen for initiation. She had still attended the Ostara ritual, but she had clearly not enjoyed it, and she'd left almost immediately after the circle was opened. In addition, Kate had been reminded of Tyler. The previous Equinox celebration had also been the first time they'd met, and she couldn't help but think about that, even though Tyler hadn't attended the ritual this time, as members of his coven had been celebrating it on their own.

"How was your ritual?" Kate asked Tyler, searching for something to talk about. "Apart from the getting-the-cold part, I mean."

"Not as good as yours was, from what I hear," Tyler told her. "Word on the street is that you, Cooper, and Annie put together a cool Equinox. What's this I hear about you making everyone pretend to be baby geese?"

Kate laughed. "That was Annie's idea," she said. "Everyone was supposed to have just hatched. You know, spring and all that."

"It sounds like fun," said Tyler.

There was a pause in the conversation as Kate, not knowing what to say, waited for Tyler to tell her why he had called.

"I didn't really call to talk about Ostara," he

said finally. "There's something else. Initiations are coming up, and I wanted to say that I hope what happened between us won't make you feel weird about maybe joining the Coven of the Green Wood."

So that's it, Kate thought. Tyler had been worried about her maybe joining the coven that he, his mother, and his sister belonged to. She had to smile to herself. She had been worried about the same thing. Ever since the idea of initiation had become a real possibility, she'd wondered if she could possibly work in the same coven as her ex.

"I know you guys are hearing about all the different covens right now," Tyler continued when Kate didn't say anything. "I think my mother and Thatcher are presenting next week, or maybe the week after. So if you think maybe we're the group for you, I just want you to know that I'm okay with that."

"Thanks," said Kate simply.

"So, *have* you thought about which coven you might want to join?" Tyler inquired.

Kate couldn't help but notice a hint of hopefulness in Tyler's voice. Did he want her to join the Coven of the Green Wood? Or was he hoping she would say that she'd decided not to? She wasn't sure exactly.

"I haven't really decided," she said finally. "The Daughters of the Cauldron sound really cool, but that's the only coven we've talked about so far. I probably won't decide until the presentations are all over."

"Oh," Tyler said, and again Kate couldn't decide if he was happy or disappointed by her response.

Again there was a silence as neither of them spoke. Finally, Kate said, "I should go. I have some homework to do."

"Okay," Tyler said, and this time he *did* sound relieved. "Well, just remember what I said."

"I will," Kate told him. "Bye."

She hung up. Then she sat on her bed, staring at the phone and thinking about the conversation she'd just had. It was like Tyler to worry that *she* might be worried about joining the Coven of the Green Wood. It made sense that he would call and tell her it was okay with him. But something else had been going on. It was almost as if he'd been *asking* her to join. Something in the tone of his voice had suggested to Kate that he would have liked to hear that she had selected the Coven of the Green Wood.

Or maybe not, she thought. It was sometimes hard to tell what Tyler was really thinking. He always wanted things to work out, always wanted everyone to be happy. Kate was pretty certain that's why he had asked her out again. She knew the idea of their relationship falling apart really upset him, and not just because it meant that they were no longer together. To Tyler it meant that something that *should* have been perfect wasn't, and Kate knew he couldn't stand that. She suspected that his desire to have everything work out had a lot to do with the fact that his parents had gone through such a nasty divorce. It had been one of the traits that had appealed to her at first and then, later, had irritated her. Sometimes Tyler just tried *too* hard to make things work out.

Is that what he's doing now? she asked herself. Was he trying to somehow get back together with her by encouraging her to join the Coven of the Green Wood? Or did he really mean it when he said that they would be able to work together without there being any tension between them? And even if he meant that, was it true? Could she indeed work in the same coven as Tyler and be able to focus on her magic?

She sighed deeply. *Who would have thought that the biggest problem about becoming a witch would be deciding whether or not to join your ex-boyfriend's coven?* she thought. If she'd been asked to list the major obstacles to choosing a coven a year ago, that one would have been way down on her list. Now, though, it was a definite issue. She liked the members of the Coven of the Green Wood. She'd enjoyed the rituals she'd done with them. If she and Tyler were still together, it probably *would* be high on her list of potential covens. But was it still 'high on the list? Was it even *on* the list? She wasn't sure.

The phone rang again and she picked it up.

"Can I just tell you what a genius you are?" Annie said, sounding very pleased.

"I take it you've heard about the wedding plans," said Kate. "You're okay with the Caterpillar thing?"

"Well, I *had* had my heart set on a lacy Victorian dress," Annie said. "But something with twelve feet is just as good. Or are they arms? I'm not sure. And are there twelve? Maybe there are twenty, or fifty. I should look this up."

"Well, I'm glad you're so into it," Kate said.

"You don't sound too glad," said Annie.

"It's not that," said Kate. "It's Tyler," she added, realizing too late that the last person she wanted to be talking about Tyler to was Annie. It had been Tyler's cheating with Annie that had precipitated their breakup in the first place.

"Oh," Annie said in a quiet voice.

"I'm sorry," Kate said. "I shouldn't have said anything. It's just that I just hung up from talking to him and it was kind of on my mind."

Annie hesitated. "Do you want to talk about it?" she asked cautiously.

Kate almost said no, but then she hesitated. She and Annie had been keeping the subject of Tyler buried pretty deeply. But maybe it was time they stopped doing that. After all, Annie was one of her best friends. And Tyler *was* a factor in Kate's decision about which coven she should join. Maybe talking about it with Annie would help.

"Yes," Kate said, deciding that it was time the two of them moved beyond the painful events that had come between them. "I do want to talk about it."

CHAPTER 4

Cooper was ten minutes late getting to the restaurant. She had spent the afternoon at Jane's house, rehearsing songs for their upcoming show at Black Eyed Susan's. Despite agreeing to do the gig, Cooper had still been a little hesitant. But after working through a couple of songs with Jane, she felt a lot better. The lyrics and their playing were really coming together, and Cooper had become so wrapped up in the music that she had lost all track of time. When she'd finally glanced at a clock, it had been ten minutes to seven. Even though she'd driven over as quickly as she could, she was still late, and she knew her father hated it when people were late. *So much for a good first impression*, she thought, then immediately wondered why *she* was worried about making a good impression on her father's date. Shouldn't the woman be worried about impressing *her*?

She walked into Shiva's Garden and looked around. The restaurant was unusual in that it had been designed to look like an enormous, overgrown garden. Potted trees and plants were everywhere, and the tables were tucked between them, making it difficult to see who was there. Normally that was part of the appeal for Cooper, but now she found it irritating as she tried to locate her dad. Finally she spotted him, at a table near the back.

"Sorry I'm late," she said as she made her way through the plants and reached the table. Seeing that her father was alone, she added, "Where's the lucky lady?"

Mr. Rivers smiled. "She had to take a phone call," he said. "Apparently they don't take too kindly to cell phones in here, so she went out onto the patio. She'll be back in a minute."

"A cell phone call," said Cooper, pulling out a chair across from her father and sitting down. "Sounds very busy and important."

Mr. Rivers raised an eyebrow. "Getting sarcastic already?" he asked.

Cooper gave him an innocent look. "Who, me?" she said.

Her father laughed. "Don't be too rough on her when she gets here," he said. "She's a nice lady."

"I'll be on my best behavior," said Cooper. "I promise."

She picked up the water glass sitting beside her plate and took a sip. The truth was, she *was* sort of intrigued to see what kind of woman her father would ask out on a date. It was difficult for Cooper to imagine him with anyone but her mother. Would this woman look like her? Would she be the same type of person? *Probably not*, Cooper told herself. *If she was, he might as well have just stayed married to Mom.*

"I know this is a little weird," Mr. Rivers said.

"A little," agreed Cooper. "But it's okay. I fully support your right to pursue romantic interests."

"I thought you weren't going to be sarcastic," her father said.

"I'm not," replied Cooper. "Scout's honor. I'm all for this."

"Thank you," Mr. Rivers said, sounding relieved. "I was sort of afraid to tell you about it."

"Why?" Cooper asked. "Is she nineteen years old or something?"

Her father laughed. "No," he said. "It's not that."

Cooper was looking around the restaurant, wondering when her father's date was going to arrive. Suddenly she noticed a familiar face walking through the maze of plants.

"Oh, Goddess," she said to her father. "Look who's here. It's that troublemaker Amanda Barclay."

Cooper watched as the newspaper reporter made her way through the restaurant. *What was Amanda Barclay doing at Shiva's Garden?* she wondered. It didn't seem like her kind of place. Then again, Cooper really couldn't imagine Amanda Barclay in *any* restaurant. The woman was barely human as far as Cooper was concerned. Several times she had caused problems for Cooper by writing stories about Cooper's life, first when Cooper had become involved in solving the murder of Elizabeth Sanger and then again when she had taken on the school board over its attempt to ban pentacles from being worn at Beecher Falls High School. Each time, Amanda had used the stories to further her own career rather than to do any actual service to anyone.

"Shouldn't she be out helping send innocent people to jail, or putting kittens to sleep or something?" Cooper said to her father. She looked at him and grinned. "Remember when you had a little crush on her?" she asked, referring to the time before Amanda had made life difficult for Cooper, when Mr. Rivers had thought the woman was an ace reporter. "I'm glad you learned your lesson about that."

Her father reddened. "Yes, well . . ." he said, and Cooper grinned. It wasn't often that she could embarrass her father, and she relished the opportunity to make him uncomfortable for a moment.

"Here I am."

Cooper looked up and saw Amanda Barclay standing beside their table. She frowned at the reporter. "So I see," she said frostily. "But I don't think anyone here ordered the hot-and-sour loser tonight."

She continued to stare at Amanda. What made the woman think that after everything she'd done she could come say hello to Cooper and her father as if they were all friends or something? Was she out of her mind? But Amanda didn't move. She just continued to look at Cooper. Cooper turned to her father for assistance.

"Um, Cooper, I'd like you to meet my date for tonight," he said quietly.

Cooper laughed. "Right," she said.

Her father didn't laugh. Neither did Amanda. Cooper looked back and forth from one to the other, waiting for the joke to arrive. But it never came. Her father was serious.

"What?" Cooper said finally.

Amanda pulled out the chair beside Mr. Rivers and sat down silently. Cooper's father looked awkwardly from the reporter to his daughter, not saying anything. Cooper, in turn, kept looking from Amanda Barclay to her father, not saying anything either. She was in shock. *No*, she thought. *You're dreaming*. That had to be it. Because there was no way her father was sitting at the same table with the reporter who had turned Cooper's life upside down on not one but two occasions. There was no way that he was sitting there with her as his *date*.

"I guess this is a little uncomfortable," Amanda said after a minute. She looked at Cooper. "But don't blame your father for not saying anything. It was my idea for him not to tell you about us right away."

Cooper let out a stifled laugh. Amanda Barclay was talking about herself and Cooper's father as if they'd been a couple for a long time. Cooper watched in horror as the reporter slid her hand over the tablecloth and took Mr. Rivers's hand in hers.

Cooper wanted to reach over and slap her hand away. *She shouldn't be touching him*, she thought.

"Are you ready to order?"

Cooper was startled out of her nightmare by the arrival of the waiter. He stood beside the table, looking at them all with a pleasant smile on his face. Cooper stared at him. She wanted to scream, "Help me! My father is under the influence of the most horrible woman in the universe!" But she couldn't even speak. She was too overcome by the awfulness of the situation to even *think* about eating.

"I think we need a few more minutes," Mr. Rivers said finally, and the waiter nodded and went away again.

"Cooper," her father said a moment later, "this is, I'm sure, a little awkward for everyone."

"No," Cooper said, taking up her menu and opening it. "It's fine." She pretended to look at the items on the menu. "The channa saag is really excellent here."

Her father didn't say anything as he and Amanda looked at their own menus. Cooper hid behind hers, not really reading it but staring at the words until they became meaningless blurs. Her head was reeling. *This just isn't happening*, she kept saying to herself. But it was happening. Every time she looked over the top of her menu she saw Amanda Barclay's face. How was she going to sit through an entire dinner with the woman? More important, how was she going to deal with seeing her over and over again if her father really was dating her? And what if they got married someday? Suddenly she felt sick to her stomach.

"Excuse me," she said, laying her menu down and standing up. "I have to go to the rest room."

"Are you all right?" asked her father, looking concerned.

"Yeah," Cooper said. "I'll be back in a minute."

She turned and walked quickly away, threading her way between the tables. As she passed the other diners, she couldn't help but notice how much most of them seemed to be enjoying themselves. It occurred to her how weird it was that people at one table could be having a wonderful time while right next to them other people could be wishing they were dead. *Like I do*, she thought. *No, I wish Amanda were dead*, she amended.

She pushed open the door of the rest room and went inside. Heading for a stall, she stepped inside and locked the door behind her, collapsing onto the toilet. There, safe from the eyes of anyone else, she started to cry. She hated crying. It made her feel weak and stupid, like a little girl who couldn't handle herself. She tried to keep the tears back, and as each one forced its way out she grew madder and madder.

"Damn it!" she said, smacking her hand against the door of the stall as the anger exploded out of her. "Damn it! Damn it! Damn it!"

It made her feel better to lash out, a reflection

of the unhappiness inside of her. How could her father be dating Amanda Barclay? How could he do that to her? She ran her hands through her hair and tried to breathe. It was as if he'd punched her right in the stomach. Even hearing about her parents' separation hadn't hurt this much.

She pulled a length of toilet paper from the roll next to her and wiped her eyes. She hoped they weren't too red. She wouldn't be able to stand it if Amanda Barclay knew that she'd been crying. *She'd probably write an article about it,* thought Cooper angrily. *I'm surprised she hasn't run in here to interview me.* She pictured the headline Amanda would put on the article: DATE'S DAUGHTER BOO-HOOS IN LOO.

She tried to calm the angry storm inside of her. She knew that being upset wasn't going to help anything. What she needed to do was figure out how to handle the situation. *You basically have two choices,* she told herself. *You can go back to the table and have dinner, or you can leave.* She thought for a minute. *I vote for leave,* she told herself.

She wiped her face once more, stood up, and unlocked the door. Glancing at herself in the mirror, she made sure that her eyes weren't *too* red and that there were no bits of toilet paper stuck to her face. Then she left the bathroom. She paused outside the door, looking back toward the table where her father and Amanda Barclay sat, waiting for her. She'd said that she'd come right back. But she couldn't do that. She couldn't sit and look at

Amanda Barclay sitting beside her father.

Instead she headed for the front of the restaurant and the door. She felt terrible running out on her father that way, but it was really the best thing to do. *Maybe not the most mature thing*, she thought as she walked out, hoping her father wouldn't see her, *but definitely the best thing*.

Once she was outside she practically ran to her car. As she pulled away from the curb and headed down the street, she couldn't help but feel as if she'd made a great escape. She tried not to think about her father and Amanda, still sitting at the table and probably wondering what was taking her so long. She knew her father would be angry and hurt. She knew, too, that they would have to have it out about the subject sooner rather than later. But not right away. Not yet.

She drove home. When she arrived at her house she went inside. Her mother was coming out of the kitchen and startled Cooper by saying, "Hi, honey. How was dinner with your dad?"

Cooper had told her mother about the dinner, at least partly. She'd told her that she was seeing her father, but she'd left out the small matter of his bringing a date along. At the time, she'd done it to protect her mother's feelings. Now she was glad she'd done it—to protect *both* their feelings. It would have been difficult enough to tell her mother about her father dating another woman; telling her that the woman was the person Cooper disliked probably more than anyone else in the known world would have been just about impossible.

On the other hand, it made the situation even worse. Having to pretend that everything was fine was almost as difficult as discussing her father's new dating life would have been. Almost, but not quite. Still, it hurt Cooper that she had to keep all of her feelings hidden from her mother. They had been talking a lot more recently, and Cooper was enjoying being able to share things with her mom. But now she had to smile and pretend that she'd had a great time.

"It was good." Cooper lied. "I had the matar paneer. Fantastic."

"You're home early," remarked her mother, looking at her watch.

"Oh, yeah," Cooper said. "Dad had some work he had to do, so we made an early night of it. But it's okay. I want to work on some songs anyway."

Her mother nodded. "Well, I'm glad you had a nice time," she said.

Cooper went upstairs to her room, leaving her mother to watch television in the living room. She shut her door, put her guitar and backpack down, and collapsed on the bed. By now her father would most definitely have figured out that she'd bailed on him. She half expected the phone to ring, with his angry voice on the other end. Part of her even wanted him to call, just so she could know that he at least understood a little bit why she hadn't been able to stay. But probably it was better if they didn't talk about it yet. She was still upset, and needed some time to cool off.

She looked at the clock. It was only 7:45. She had to think of something to do or she was going to just sit there and drive herself crazy. She wished she could go hang out with T.J., but he and Schroedinger's Cat were playing at someone's party. Jane had said she was going to a movie with another friend, and Kate and Annie both had other plans. Cooper was all by herself. That thought depressed her. Then, a moment later, it made her laugh.

"A year ago you would have been thrilled to be alone," she said, scolding herself. "See what happens when you let yourself make friends?"

She sat up. It was true, she had gotten so used to having Kate, Annie, T.J., and now Jane around to do things with that suddenly finding herself alone was a shock. What had she done with herself before them? What had she done up there in her room all by herself? At the time, she'd thought she was being totally independent and cool. Now she just wondered what she'd done to keep from going stir-crazy.

You wrote songs, she reminded herself. True, but now she did that with Jane and sometimes with T.J. Although she still wrote by herself quite a bit, she no longer spent hour after hour penning angry lyrics and listening to herself play guitar through her headphones. That had been her way of shutting out the world, keeping herself safe. But bit by bit she'd allowed herself to let the world in, first by becoming friends with Annie and Kate and then by dating T.J. Those things had really helped her grow. But now she felt as if they'd also opened her up to a whole new set of problems. Was she too dependent on her friends and her boyfriend? Had she let them take over *too* much of her life?

No, she told herself. *You're just afraid that you're losing them. And you're afraid you're losing your father, too.*

Suddenly it all fell into place for her. Sure, she'd reacted so strongly to seeing her father with Amanda Barclay because she hated the woman. But it was more than that. It had reminded her of everything else she seemed to be losing. After being a loner for so long, she'd finally made some real friends. But now Kate and Annie were moving on without her, joining covens and becoming real witches while she had to be content with working on her own. She'd let T.J. into her life, and now she had to face the very real possibility that in a little more than a year they might be pulled apart by college. It was as if all of the connections she'd so hesitantly made were being torn apart, just as she'd always feared they would be.

Cooper's thoughts went back to the night of her dedication ceremony. *Connection* had been the word she'd drawn from the cauldron, the word that was supposed to represent her primary challenge for the coming year and a day. Well, she'd met that challenge head-on. But where had it gotten her? *I'm in my room, alone, on a Friday night*, she thought bitterly. *So much for that little bit of magic.* Even her connection to Wicca was being taken away from her now that she was essentially being excluded from the covens. But why? Why was everything she'd worked so hard for being jerked out from under her?

Her eyes went to the altar beside her bed, and the image of the Goddess that sat on it. Ever since being turned down for initiation, Cooper hadn't devoted any time to her witchcraft studies. She was too depressed. Now she stared at the statue.

"I don't get it," she said. "What did I ever do to you?"

She waited a moment, as if expecting the statue to answer her. Then she sighed. "Might as well get started on my homework," she said, looking at the schoolbooks piled on her desk and wondering if her life could possibly get any worse than it was.

CHAPTER 5

"Well, what do you think?"

Annie took the paint chip and looked at it. "It's really yellow," she said.

Becka sighed. "I know," she said. "I want some color, but I can't decide what would look the best in that room."

"Maybe you should go a little darker," Annie suggested, selecting another chip. "What about this? It's called Curried Peach."

Becka made a face. "What's with these names?" she asked. "The last one was Summerlight. Do they really think people pick colors based on the names?"

Annie laughed. "Why not?" she replied. "J. Crew operates on the same principle."

They were standing in the paint section of the local home improvement store, staring blankly at the rows and rows of paint color chips. Grayson and Becka had unexpectedly been able to come up for the weekend, and they'd decided that it would be the perfect time for Becka to paint the room that was going to be hers. She and Annie had been sent to the store on Saturday morning to get the paint. They'd been looking at colors for half an hour, and Becka still hadn't been able to choose one. Now she groaned.

"Let's just paint it off-white," she said.

"No way!" exclaimed Annie. "If you do that I'm never visiting you in your room. Now, let's focus. What's your favorite color?"

"Black," Becka said.

"Well, that's out," Annie told her. "So we have to come up with something else."

"Tell you what," said Becka. "How about I let *you* pick it?"

"Me?" Annie said.

"Surprise me," said Becka. "I'll go get brushes and drop cloths and stuff. You get the paint. When we get home I'll see what you came up with."

"But what if you hate it?" Annie said. "Then we'll have to do this all over again."

"I trust you," Becka told her. "See you in twenty."

She turned and disappeared down the aisle where the painting accessories were. Left alone, Annie stood and looked at the vast array of color choices displayed on the wall. What was she going to pick for her soon-to-be-sort-of-sister's room? She wanted it to be something cool, something Becka would really love. But what color did you choose for a girl who liked black? Annie looked at her watch. *Sixteen minutes to go*, she thought.

She thought about her own room. It was painted a dark honey color that lit up when the sun filled the room. Looking at it made Annie feel like she was in a warm, golden cocoon. She wanted Becka to feel the same way when she was in her new room. But what color would make someone like Becka feel at home? Annie scanned the rows of colors, and suddenly her eyes stopped at one in particular.

No, she thought. *I couldn't. That is so* not *Becka*.

She moved on to different colors, but time and again she returned to the one that had grabbed her attention. Each time she rejected it again, knowing that it would be disastrous. But then she was brought right back to it again. It was as if some other force was making her pay attention to that one paint chip. Finally, she reached out and took it.

She's going to kill me, she thought as she examined the chip, holding it up to the light. But over and over again her study of Wicca had taught her to trust her instincts, and she decided to go for it. *Besides*, she thought as she grabbed two gallons of paint and headed for the color-processing counter, *it's not like I have to live with it*.

When Becka joined her ten minutes later, her arms laden with rollers and brushes, Annie held up the cans of paint. "Ta da," she said dramatically.

"I can't wait to see it," said Becka as they headed for the checkout counter. "Is it something cool?"

"It's something, all right," Annie said mysteriously. "You'll see."

An hour later they were standing in the center of what was now Becka's bedroom. They'd removed all of the junk that had been stored there, vacuumed out all of the dust, put a drop cloth over the wood floor, and taped around the edges. Both girls were dressed in old clothes, and Becka was standing in front of Annie, who was kneeling on the floor and prying the lid off the first can of paint. Finally she got it off and showed Becka the color she'd chosen.

"Pink?" Becka said, surprised.

"Not just pink," Annie told her. "Venetian Pink." She looked at Becka hopefully. "I think it's supposed to remind you of Italy for some reason. What do you think?"

"I think it's pink," Becka said carefully. She had a peculiar expression on her face.

"You hate it," said Annie. "It's okay. We can take it back. I don't know why I picked this color. Something kept bringing me back to it. But I know it isn't really you, and I should have gone for the blue I liked in the first place." She began to put the lid back on the paint.

"No," Becka said, stopping her. "It's okay."

Annie looked up at her. "It is?" she asked doubtfully.

Becka nodded. "I just don't know how you knew," she said.

"Knew what?" Annie asked her, confused. "I

don't know why I picked it. Honestly. It's like it just wouldn't go away."

Becka smiled and laughed. "That was my mom's favorite color," she said. "In a lot of the pictures I have of her she's wearing it. I always wanted to paint my room that color but I was afraid it would freak my dad out. Plus, I thought people would think I was way too girly," she added.

"Great," Annie said, the momentary happiness that had welled up in her draining right back out again. "So now I'm going to give your dad a fit and make you feel like you're six."

"No," said Becka, dipping a brush in the paint and applying a little of it to the wall, where it immediately made the room feel brighter and airier. "I like it. And I think my dad will like it, too."

"It reminded me of the roses my mother used to grow," said Annie. "You know, the ones that used to cover the porch of our house—of your house. One of them is planted in the garden here now."

"This is our house now," Becka replied thoughtfully, adding more paint to the wall in broad strokes. Annie joined her, using the roller, and soon they had one entire wall done. As Becka painted the edges, Annie filled in the large spaces in between, and working as a team they had most of the room done in no time. When it was almost complete they took a break and looked at their handiwork.

"You know, I was kind of worried about moving here," Becka told Annie.

"Worried?" Annie asked.

Becka nodded. "I was afraid you would feel like I was taking away some of your space," she said. "You know, you have this whole floor to yourself. Now I'll be here. I know we talk about how much fun it will be, but part of me was worried that you might not like having another sister after all."

"And now?" said Annie.

Becka looked at the walls of her room, glowing pink in the late-morning sun. "I think anyone who would dare pick this color for me is exactly the kind of sister I want to have," she said.

"Remember that when we're both trying to use the bathroom in the morning," Annie told her.

They finished the rest of the room and then left it to dry. Going downstairs, they found Aunt Sarah, Grayson, and Meg in the kitchen, putting out sandwich makings.

"Perfect timing," Aunt Sarah said as the girls arrived. "We were just going to call you."

"How goes the painting?" asked Mr. Dunning.

"The first coat is done," Becka told him. "We'll do the second one this afternoon and that's it."

"And what was the final color choice?" Aunt Sarah asked them as she sliced a tomato for her sandwich.

Becka looked at Annie. "We're keeping that a surprise," Becka said. "You can see it when it's done."

"They're already teaming up against us," Grayson

said to Aunt Sarah. "We're doomed."

"I'm already used to getting it from my two," Annie's aunt told him. "You're the one who's going to be experiencing having more than one girl around. And if you really think about it, there will be *four* of us against you from time to time."

Becka's father looked at the radiant faces of his daughter, his fiancée, and her two nieces as they all smiled at him. "I hadn't thought of that until just now," he said, laughing nervously.

"Well, it's too late to back out," Aunt Sarah told him. "We've got costumes ordered." She turned to Becka and Annie. "I spoke to Juliet today," she said. "She and her friends are thrilled about making the costumes for the wedding. They're starting this weekend."

Annie's aunt had broached the subject of the *Alice in Wonderland* wedding with Grayson as soon as he'd arrived the night before. To Annie's delight, he had agreed immediately, finding it a wonderful idea. After some discussion it had been decided that he and Aunt Sarah would indeed be Alice and the Mad Hatter. Meg was the White Rabbit, finding the Dormouse—in her words—"a total snore," and Becka had agreed to dress as the Cheshire Cat, but only after trying valiantly to persuade her father and Aunt Sarah to let her go as the more fearsome Jabberwocky. They had vetoed that suggestion, Grayson telling her that the wedding was going to be "brillig enough" without the addition of monsters.

Annie, who had been quite looking forward to going as the Caterpillar, was the only one whose costume seemed potentially impossible. Her aunt had decided to wait until speaking with Juliet to see what her thoughts on the subject were before deciding on Annie's final getup. Now Annie waited breathlessly to hear her fate. She was afraid that if the Caterpillar idea had to be nixed she'd end up as something awful, like one of the talking flowers, or perhaps the Walrus or the Carpenter.

"And you'll be happy to know that Juliet thinks she can do something very interesting with your Caterpillar outfit," Aunt Sarah said finally, making Annie breathe a sigh of relief. "She even has an idea for making movable arms, which, frankly, I find a little creepy."

"No, it will be really cool," Annie said. "The more arms the better."

"I'm getting whiskers," Meg said happily. "And a waistcoat. Grayson said I can even wear his father's pocket watch."

Annie began making herself a lettuce, cheese, and tomato sandwich. "This wedding is going to be perfect," she remarked.

"I must say, it *does* all seem to be coming together remarkably well," said Aunt Sarah. "I keep waiting for one of those disasters all the wedding planning books tell you to expect, but so far it looks as if it's going to be smooth sailing."

They all gathered around the kitchen table and

ate. Watching everyone, Annie realized that for the first time since she was a little girl, she felt as if she was having a real family meal. With her aunt on one side and Grayson on the other, it reminded her of sitting at the table with her parents. She used to love sitting between them, eating her lunch or her dinner and listening to them talk. She'd felt secure then, and loved.

Not that she hadn't felt loved since then, or that she hadn't felt part of a family. Her aunt and her sister were definitely her family. So were Kate and Cooper. But there was something about being part of a complete circle again. It was as if Grayson and Becka had been missing from their lives, and now that they were all together something very, very special had been formed.

This is what I want my coven to feel like, Annie thought. *I want it to feel like family.* She watched the faces around the table as they ate and talked. Each of them was unique. She looked at Meg, carefully cutting the crusts from her egg salad sandwich before eating it, then at Becka, who, she now noticed, alternated bites of her sandwich with sips from her glass. Her aunt, chatting away amiably, made sure that none of the different foods on her plate touched, while Grayson basically pushed everything into a big pile and went at it enthusiastically, scooping up potato salad with the bread from his sandwich. Annie herself had a habit of never eating food that crunched too much, because the texture bothered her.

Noting the little eccentricities each of them possessed, Annie realized that each of them brought something different to the family group. She, her aunt, and Meg had lived with each other for so long that they had become accustomed to each other. But now that Becka and Grayson were going to be part of their family, how would that change things? Would the familiar pattern of life in the Crandall household be disrupted now that it was the Crandall-Dunning household? Or would it become something new, a combination of the two? What would happen, for example, if her aunt discovered that Grayson always left the top off the toothpaste tube, or if Annie and Becka clashed over the issue of eating peanut butter right out of the jar?

It's like making magic with other people, thought Annie as she chewed her sandwich. She, Kate, and Cooper had sometimes clashed over their differing styles of doing things. But they'd always managed to work things out, and the magic they'd made as a result of compromising and respecting one another's views had been more powerful than anything any of them could do on their own.

So maybe I don't need to be in a coven with people just like me, Annie realized. In thinking about where she would find the best home for her Wiccan work, she had been assuming that she should look for a coven of people like herself. But perhaps that was the wrong approach. Maybe, instead, she should look for a coven that had a lot of diversity in it. But was there one? So far they'd only heard about the Daughters of the Cauldron. Annie would have to wait to see who they heard from next.

When lunch was over Annie and Becka went back upstairs to see how the bedroom looked now that they'd been away from it for a while. The paint had dried, and it was slightly lighter than it had appeared going on. The effect made the room look like it had been warmed by the sun for many years.

"It really does look like the pink color you see in Italian frescoes, doesn't it?" Becka remarked as they stood admiring their work. "My dad has a photo book of them, and this is exactly what some of them look like."

"So maybe whoever picks those paint names actually got one right," said Annie.

"I think one more coat to cover everything again and we'll be done," Becka told her.

They got back to work. This time things went even more quickly, as they could more easily see which areas needed attention. Once again working as a team, but with Annie doing the trim work and Becka wielding the roller, they had soon finished. When they were done Becka rubbed at a spot of pink that had gotten on her cheek. "I think after all of this we deserve some fun tonight," she said. "Think the girls are up for a night out?"

"Let's find out," said Annie.

A few phone calls later, they'd gotten acceptances

from Kate, Cooper, and Sasha. Cooper was going to see if Jane wanted to join them as well.

"Now we just have to agree on where to eat and what to do," Annie told Becka. "But at least we know we're doing it at six."

"That gives us a couple of hours to get ready," said Becka. "I for one am in desperate need of a shower."

"Same here," Annie said. "Why don't you go first. I'll clean up in the bedroom."

Becka disappeared into the bathroom while Annie returned to the bedroom and began putting the lids back on the cans and gathering up the painting supplies. She pulled the masking tape away from the window edges and the baseboards, and pulled up the tarps. Then she took all of it downstairs and put it in the big garage behind the house.

Back upstairs, she stood in the newly painted bedroom and listened to the water running in the bathroom between her room and Becka's. She could hear Becka singing. She also heard the voices of her aunt and Grayson coming from the kitchen downstairs.

This house feels more alive than it has in a long time, she thought happily. *Now if I can just find a coven that feels the same way, I'll be totally happy.*

CHAPTER 6

"Look at this one." Kate's Aunt Netty handed her another photograph.

Kate and her aunt were sitting at a table in a restaurant on Sunday afternoon. Netty had called that morning to say she was coming by for a visit, which had delighted her niece. Kate hadn't seen her aunt in more than a month, and she was looking forward to it. When Netty had added that she had a surprise for Kate, that had just upped the excitement level.

Now, waiting for their food to arrive, Kate was finding out what the surprise was. She looked at the image in her hand. It depicted a circle of women dressed in white and wearing garlands of flowers in their hair. They were standing in front of some enormous stones, and their arms were held up to the sky.

"That's an Ostara ritual in England," Netty told Kate. "That coven has been in existence for almost seventy years. That woman in the center has been in it for almost sixty. Her mother was the founder."

Kate put the photograph next to the other ones her aunt had brought. All of them depicted women participating in rituals of one kind or another. There were pictures taken at a pagan women's weekend retreat, where the women all painted their bodies in bright colors and danced around a fire. There were some showing women clad in black robes standing waist-deep in the ocean and pouring water from their hands into the sea. Another focused on the radiant face of a woman dressed as the goddess Kali during a celebration.

"These are gorgeous," Kate said to her aunt. "I can't believe you didn't tell me you were doing this."

Netty shrugged. "I didn't want to say too much about it," she replied. "You know, in case it didn't work out. But bit by bit over the last six months it's really been coming together. Whenever I go on an assignment somewhere I see if I can locate Wiccan groups in the area and photograph them. I've met some really amazing people."

"What are you going to do with them all?" Kate asked.

"A book," said her aunt. "I want to do a photo book about women and Wiccan spirituality."

Kate's eyes lit up. "That's a fantastic idea!" she said. "People would love to see these pictures."

"That's what I'm hoping," said her aunt as she began gathering up the pile of photographs. "I'm going to start putting together a proposal for it. Sophia is going to help me. Then I'm going to show it to some of the editors I know through my magazine work and see if I can't get something happening."

Kate helped Netty put the images away. She was so proud of her aunt. Ever since first meeting Sophia and the other witches who had helped perform a healing ritual for her when she was battling cancer, Netty had gotten more and more interested in Wicca. She had been attending rituals with a group near her home, and she and Sophia had become good friends. Now she was using her photography skills to combine her interest in the Craft with her professional life.

"I almost forgot to tell you," said Netty as she zipped up the portfolio in which she'd carried the photographs. "I'm a novice in my coven."

"No way!" Kate exclaimed.

Her aunt nodded. "They said I was hanging around so much it was either that or make me their mascot," Netty joked. "So I decided to officially join. They have this training program you do, after which you become a full member. They pair you up with an older witch in the group, and that person is kind of like your teacher until they feel you're ready. I'm working with this great woman. She's been a witch for thirty years, and she's also a doctor. She loves that I had cancer. I guess she's always trying to get her patients to try alternative approaches to healing. She says she's going to use me for show-and-tell one of these days."

Kate laughed. She looked at her aunt's smiling

face. It was hard to believe that less than a year earlier they had been afraid that Netty would die. At the time, Kate would never have believed that her aunt would be sitting across the table from her, showing her pictures she'd taken of women involved in witchcraft. Kate had been afraid to even say the word *witch* to her family then. But now both she and her aunt were deeply involved in Wicca.

"Now tell me about you," Netty said. "What's happening with initiation?"

Kate took a sip of her drink. "It's weird," she said. "It feels like when they have pledge week at the university and all the fraternities and sororities recruit the freshmen. We're learning about some of the different covens there are around here. Then we're supposed to pick the one we think we'll fit into the best. I thought we'd all just be initiated into the coven Sophia is in."

Her aunt laughed. "She mentioned that they were trying something new this year," she said. "But I think it's smart. No coven can be perfect for everyone. I went to rituals held by three or four different ones before I settled on the Coven of the Waxing Moon."

"Why did you pick them?" Kate asked.

"It was just a feeling I had," replied her aunt. "The first coven I met was too formal. I was always afraid I was going to do something wrong during their rituals. It felt like being in school. The others I tried were okay, but nothing special. Then I went to a full moon circle held by the coven I'm in now, and it just felt right. I liked the energy. Plus, they had *great* snacks afterward."

"Which is key to working good magic," said Kate seriously, making her aunt laugh. "I guess that's how I'll decide where I want to go, too," she added.

"Are you leaning one way or another?" her aunt inquired.

"I really like Sophia and Archer and the women from the store," Kate said after a moment. "They're all really great."

"But," her aunt said when Kate hesitated.

Kate shrugged. "I don't know," she said. "I feel sort of like a traitor saying this, because they've been so great and everything, but I don't know if I fit in with them." She looked at her aunt. "Don't take this personally or anything, but most of them are a lot older than I am."

Netty pretended to be horrified. "I can't believe you'd say such a thing," she said. "Why, they're the same age as I am."

Kate rolled her eyes at her aunt's dramatic statement. "That's the point," Kate said. "I'm afraid I would always think of them as teachers. You know, instead of friends."

"But you and I are friends," Netty reminded her. "Even if I am your ancient auntie who's about to crumble to dust at any second."

"I'm sorry I mentioned it," Kate said sarcastically. "I *know* they aren't that old. And I know you and I

71

are friends. I think of Sophia as a friend, too. But not the same way I think of, say, Annie and Cooper as friends. When we do magic together it's like we're all learning together. There's something really cool about that. We're all going through a lot of the same stuff, with school and boyfriends and parents and all of that."

"Are you saying you would like to be in a circle of all young people?" asked Netty.

"No," Kate answered quickly. "I know we need more experienced people to teach us. But I'd like to find a coven that has some of that newness to it."

Her aunt was nodding. "I get it," she said. "So, what are your other options?"

"I don't know yet," Kate said. "I'm waiting to find out. The only other group I know of right now is the Coven of the Green Wood."

"The one Tyler is in," her aunt said.

Kate nodded. "Right."

"And so that's not an option?" Netty asked.

Kate screwed up her face in a look of thought-fulness. "I don't think it's not an option," she said carefully. "Tyler has already said he wouldn't have a problem about it."

"But would *you* have a problem with it?" her aunt inquired gently.

"The jury is out on that one," Kate told her. "The Coven of the Green Wood does have some young people in it. Tyler and his sister, for starters. And I like a lot of the people in it."

"Mmm-hmm," Netty remarked. "But could you work magic with your ex-boyfriend?"

"I don't know," Kate replied. "Honestly? I think it would be weird."

Her aunt didn't say anything. Kate knew that Netty was attempting to remain neutral. She also knew that remaining neutral was practically impossible for her aunt.

"What do *you* think?" she asked Netty, seeing if she could get her to crack.

"I think our lunch is here," Netty replied, clearly relieved to see the waiter arriving with their food.

"Good save," Kate told her as the waiter set their plates down. "But I'm not letting you off the hook. What do you think?"

Netty picked up her fork and jabbed it into her salad. She held up a lettuce leaf and waved it at Kate. "I think that for once I'm staying out of it."

"Come on!" Kate wailed. "You're supposed to be my all-knowing aunt. My *beautiful* aunt," she added.

Netty snorted. "Now you're pushing it," she said. "If you'd said smart, or talented, you might have had me."

Kate groaned. "At least give me *something*," she implored.

"Okay," Netty said. "Here's what I think. I think that you've learned a lot in the last year. I think that you've found out a lot about who you are as a person. I think that you've learned to trust your instincts. So trust them."

"*That* is your advice?" Kate said, glaring at her aunt over her sandwich.

"Fine," Netty told her. "Don't take it. Why don't you just do whatever your friends are doing? That would make it easy for you."

"Not really," Kate said. "For one thing, Cooper isn't being initiated."

It was her aunt's turn to be shocked. "What?" she said in bewilderment.

"They said she's not ready," Kate explained.

"How's she taking it?" asked her aunt, chewing a crouton.

"Like Cooper," said Kate. "She's pretending it's fine, which means she's basically pretending it didn't happen."

"I'm so sorry to hear that," Netty said. "It must be making things hard for the three of you."

"It's not making it easy," admitted Kate.

"And what about Annie?" asked Netty. "Has she said what she wants to do?"

Kate shook her head. "I think she likes the idea of joining the Daughters of the Cauldron," she answered. "But we haven't talked about it a lot. She's been busy with her aunt's wedding and getting the house ready and all of that."

Her aunt put down her fork. "Hey," she said, suddenly sounding concerned. "Is something wrong?"

Kate sighed and poked at her sandwich. "I don't know," she said. "Things just don't feel quite right."

"Things?" Netty said.

"Yeah," said Kate. "I guess it's that I had this idea of how everything would be when this time came, and now things are totally different. Cooper isn't being initiated. Annie has this whole new family coming. And I'm sort of left in the middle."

Now that she'd started speaking, Kate found herself pouring out her feelings to her aunt, feelings she hadn't even realized were building up inside of her.

"Last year when I thought about initiation I pictured the three of us doing it together. Then I imagined us all doing rituals with the coven. Me, Annie, Cooper . . . and Tyler," she concluded.

"But now that isn't happening," her aunt said.

"No," Kate said. "Tyler and I aren't together. Cooper, Annie, and I aren't together. It's just all . . . different."

"Different isn't necessarily bad," her aunt told her after a moment. "Contrary to what the fairy tales tell you, life doesn't usually work out the way you expect it to. Some days you wake up and find out you have cancer, or that the person you love doesn't love you back. Plans fall apart. Directions change." She looked at her niece. "But those aren't always bad things. Sometimes they make you go down a road you would never have considered, and sometimes you find something really wonderful waiting for you there."

Kate looked at Netty. She knew her aunt was

right. *Look at her,* Kate told herself. *She could have let the cancer destroy her life. But she didn't, and now she's doing this cool photography project. And you're whining because you have to choose which coven to join?* When she put it that way, her problems seemed kind of stupid. But they didn't *feel* stupid to her. They felt very real.

"I remember coming home from my doctor's office the day I found out I had cancer," her aunt told her. "I sat on the couch and I looked at the pictures on my mantelpiece—pictures of my friends, pictures of you and Kyle and your parents. I got really angry, and not because I was upset that I might never see you all again."

Kate looked at her aunt, not understanding.

"I was angry because you were going to get to have lives that I wasn't going to get to have," her aunt said. "I know that probably sounds very selfish, and I suppose it was. But I couldn't help but think that you were all going to have a lot more years of feeling the sun on your faces, and smelling bread baking, and opening birthday presents. Maybe you would get married and have children. You were going to get to do things that I wouldn't get to do. Never mind that some of those things I didn't even *want* to do," she added, smiling softly. "The point was that I was angry that the life I had planned for myself was being taken away from me."

Netty stopped talking and went back to eating her salad. Kate thought about what her aunt had said. "It's not so much that I think things are being taken away," she said. "It's more like I thought that studying Wicca was going to bring Annie, Cooper, and me closer together. Now it seems almost like it's forcing us apart."

"It's all about change," her aunt said. "And believe me, there's a reason for all of it. There's a reason I got cancer, and there's a reason I beat it. There's a reason you met Tyler, there's a reason you broke up, and there's a reason you're being asked to decide whether or not you want to work in a coven with him now. You might not see those reasons, but they're there."

Kate took a bite of her sandwich and chewed it while she thought. It seemed to her that ever since she'd first opened the book of spells that had started her on her journey into Wicca, she'd been asked to make one difficult decision after another. She'd had to decide whether to remain friends with Sherrie and the other girls she'd hung out with, she'd had to decide what to tell her family about her involvement in Wicca, and she'd had to decide whether to stay with her old boyfriend or start dating Tyler. And those were just the first of many more hard choices she'd been asked to make.

And here I thought that studying witchcraft was supposed to make life easier, she thought. Instead, it seemed like the more she allowed the Craft to influence her life, the more it demanded of her.

Yes, she argued with herself. *But look how much you've learned.*

That was true. She had become a much different person because of her involvement with Wicca. She had become stronger, more confident. She had learned that she could face challenges and overcome them using her strengths. She had stopped being a person who worried what other people thought of her—at least most of the time. She had learned the power to be found in standing up for what she believed in. And she had learned the joy of being part of something that connected her to other people in a meaningful way.

Okay, she thought. *Enough with the Oprah-esque pep talk. You still haven't solved your basic problem, which is what you want to do about this coven business.*

She finished her sandwich in silence, thinking about everything she and her aunt had discussed. Then, as the waiter came to clear away their plates, Netty said, "You know what else I learned from having cancer?"

"What's that?" Kate asked, preparing herself to hear another deep statement.

Her aunt waved the dessert menu at Kate. "That there's very little that a brownie with hot fudge and vanilla ice cream can't solve."

Kate laughed, feeling better than she had a moment before. "Better make it *two* scoops of ice cream," she said.

CHAPTER 7

"So he never called?" Jane asked Cooper. It was Monday night, and Cooper had gone over to the Goldsteins' to practice. She and Jane had been discussing the disastrous dinner Cooper had had—or rather, had *not* had—with her father and Amanda Barclay on Friday night.

"Not a word," Cooper said. "Of course, I haven't exactly been answering the phone either. And he won't leave a message, not if he thinks my mother might hear it."

Jane strummed her guitar idly for a few moments. "Do you think you'd be as mad if it was someone else and not this reporter woman?" she asked.

"No," Cooper said instantly. "If he wants to date, that's his problem."

Jane grinned. "*That* was sort of hostile," she said.

Cooper sighed. "Fine. So maybe I'm not thrilled about the idea of my dad dating right now. But did he have to go and pick the most obnoxious woman who ever wrote a newspaper article?" She gave Jane a meaningful look. "I don't even think she's human," she said seriously.

Jane let out a laugh. "Next you'll be telling me she sleeps in a coffin and is terrified of garlic," she remarked.

"I wish," said Cooper. "Then I'd know how to get rid of her. One good stake to the heart and the whole problem would be over."

"How long do you plan on punishing your dad?" asked Jane.

"I'm not punishing him," said Cooper irritably. "I just don't know what to say to him." She turned to her friend. "And what's with making everything about me lately, anyway?" she demanded. "What about *you*?"

"What about me?" Jane asked casually.

"How's the whole lesbian thing working out?" asked Cooper, trying not to grin.

"It's *fine*," replied Jane. "Thank you for asking. And by the way, I think I prefer *gay*, not *lesbian*. *Lesbian* sounds like something you put on toast. You know, like 'Could you please pass the lesbian.'" She made a shuddering gesture. "It makes me feel like preserves."

"Okay, so you're gay," Cooper said. "Whatever. The real question is, have you met any hot chicks?"

"Hot chicks?" Jane repeated. "You sound like some football player in a locker room."

"You're avoiding the question," Cooper retorted. "Which probably means you *have* met a hot chick and you just don't want me to know about it."

Jane reddened. "Okay," she said. "I give. There is this girl in my support group at the center."

"I knew it," Cooper said happily. "Tell me everything."

Jane suddenly looked embarrassed. "I don't know," she said. "She's just this girl."

"What's her name?" Cooper asked impatiently.

"Siobhan," answered Jane.

"Oh, an Irish girl," said Cooper. "Sounds cute. Is she?"

Jane blushed even more. "I guess," she said.

"Are you going to make me pull every single detail out of you?" Cooper demanded. "Fine. We'll start with her hair. What color is it?"

"Red," Jane said, then said, "brown. Well, reddish brown."

"Long or short? Her hair, I mean."

"Short."

"Eyes?"

"Greenish."

"Height?"

"A little shorter than me."

"Piercings?"

"Just ears."

"Tattoos?"

"No."

"Favorite band?"

"Eve 6."

"Good kisser?"

"Ye— Hey!"

"Got you!" Cooper howled in triumph. "So you've kissed her. Way to go."

Jane covered her face with her hands. "It was just once!" she wailed as Cooper hooted with laughter. "Okay, twice."

"Jane has a girlfriend," Cooper said in a singsong voice.

"She's not my girlfriend," said Jane emphatically. "We're just hanging out."

"Well, when are you going to bring her around to hang out with the rest of us?" asked Cooper.

"Oh, I don't know," replied Jane doubtfully. "I don't know if she's ready for that."

"She's not out?" asked Cooper, sounding sympathetic.

"Oh, she's out," Jane said. "I just don't know if I want to expose her to the evil influence of you and the rest of the gang."

"Ha ha," Cooper said. "Seriously, are we going to meet her?"

"Maybe," said Jane. "I'm thinking of asking her to come hear us play on Friday. But you guys have to promise to behave yourselves."

"Us?" Cooper said, sounding shocked. "What would we do?"

"Who knows?" answered Jane. "Pretty much anything."

Cooper held her hand over her heart. "I swear, we'll be perfect angels," she said. Then she grinned. "Well, mostly."

"Yeah, well, it's the other side of mostly that I'm worried about," Jane said. "I told my parents about her," she added more seriously.

"Get out," exclaimed Cooper. "And?"

"And not much," said Jane. "They just sort of nodded and smiled. I think we've entered the 'If we don't say too much maybe she'll forget she's gay' phase of their acceptance. They did the same thing when I told them I wanted a pony."

"Well, I'm really proud of you for telling them," said Cooper.

"Thanks, Mom," Jane said.

"Seriously," Cooper told her. "It's a big deal. Take it from someone who knows a thing or two about not communicating with parents, you did good."

"I know," Jane said. "And it does feel good. I feel like for the first time in my life I'm really expressing who I am. It's so nice not to feel trapped anymore." She paused. "Siobhan comes from such a different situation," she said. "Her dad is gay, so she had someone to talk to about it. Not that her mom was exactly wild about the idea, but at least she'd been through it all before with Siobhan's dad. Now she calls him her dress rehearsal."

"I don't think anyone really gets an easy deal," Cooper told her. "It's just that some people's lives *look* easier from the outside. We all have our own stuff to deal with."

"Speaking of dealing with stuff, how are you

about the whole initiation thing these days?" Jane asked her.

"I think I feel about that the way your parents felt about the pony," Cooper answered. "The less I talk about it, the more I can pretend it's not there."

"Sorry," said Jane. "I didn't mean to remind you. It's just that I sort of had an idea about it."

Cooper hesitated. She really didn't want to talk about the initiation nightmare anymore. But Jane had been very open with her about Siobhan, and Cooper felt like she was letting her friend down by not being as willing to discuss her own feelings. *After all,* she told herself, *her situation is a lot harder to deal with than mine is.*

"What kind of idea?" she said finally.

Jane put down her guitar and went to her bookshelf. She came back carrying a small book, which she handed to Cooper. It was called *Witch Alone: A Handbook for Solitaries.* "I picked this up at the used book store downtown," she said. "It looked interesting."

Cooper opened the book and thumbed through it. It appeared to be a guide for people interested in Wicca who either couldn't find a coven or preferred not to work with one. There were chapters on creating rituals, celebrating the sabbats, and other topics familiar to Cooper from her studies.

"I know you already know most of the stuff in there," said Jane. "That's not why I got it for you. The part I thought you might find interesting is the chapter on self-initiation."

"Self-initiation?" said Cooper.

Jane nodded. "The author doesn't believe that witches have to be initiated by other witches," she explained. "After all, that would mean that someone somewhere was the first witch and started the whole thing, and anyone who couldn't trace her lineage back to that person must not be a real witch, and that's just stupid."

"We talked about that in class," Cooper said. "There are people who claim to be able to trace the history of their covens back hundreds of years, but none of them can actually prove it."

"Right," Jane said. "Well, that's pretty much what this guy says. He says that nobody has to tell you you're a witch for you to be one. It's not like getting a license or something."

Cooper laughed. "I'd like to see the test for that," she joked.

"He's right, though," Jane continued. "I mean, who's to say whether you're really a witch or not? If you accept the basic beliefs of Wicca, and if you're dedicated to living your life based on those principles, doesn't that make you a witch?"

Cooper thought about that for a minute as she flipped through the book some more. That hadn't occurred to her. She'd been so focused on the concept of initiation, and on what that meant, that she hadn't stopped to think that maybe it didn't really mean anything at all, at least not when it came to what she believed and how she lived her life.

"I guess the whole initiation thing is just a ceremony, really," she said.

"Then is there any reason why you can't do it for yourself?" asked Jane.

Cooper looked at her. "I don't know," she said honestly.

"He gives some ideas for self-dedication rituals in there," Jane told her. "I don't know, maybe it's something to think about."

Cooper looked at the book in her hands. Part of her was grateful to Jane for thinking of her. But another part—the larger and noisier part—was ashamed that she was even having to consider the idea of self-initiation. She didn't know why, really, but it made her feel like she was taking the easier road or buying a knockoff of something because she couldn't get the real thing. Still, she didn't want to make Jane feel bad for bringing it up.

"Thanks," she said. "I'll look at this later." She put the book into her backpack. "But right now we have got to get working on these songs," she said, trying to sound enthusiastic. "We've got to have them down by Friday night."

They returned to their music, concentrating on polishing the material they'd been working on. After an hour or so Cooper looked at Jane. "I think we're ready," she said. "How about one more practice later this week?"

"Sounds good to me," Jane replied. "Do you think Betty Bangs will love us?"

Cooper waved her hand at Jane. "Love us?" she said. "She's going to beg us to let her sing with us."

Jane looked thoughtful. "That gives me an idea," she said. "What if we throw a Scrapple song into the set?"

"Trying to get on the judge's good side," Cooper said. "I like that. Which one did you have in mind?"

"What about 'Angry on the Outside'?" Jane suggested.

Cooper shook her head. "Not one of my favorites," she said. "How about 'What You Said'?"

Jane considered it for a moment. "Not enough harmony parts," she said. "We need something we can both really wail on."

The two of them thought silently for a minute. Then Cooper looked at Jane. "'Song for a Tired Girl,'" they said in unison.

"That's perfect," Jane said. "It's got a great guitar part, the lyrics are fantastic, and we can both sing on it."

"Betty will love it," agreed Cooper.

"We'll practice it next time," Jane said. "We should do this plugged in instead of acoustic, though. Can we do it at your place? My mother's convinced we'll set off my grandfather's pacemaker or something if we play electric here."

"No problem," Cooper answered. "I'll call you later about a time, okay?"

She picked up her stuff and Jane walked her to the door. A few minutes later she was heading home. The car stereo was turned up and she was singing along to the music. But singing wasn't what was really on her mind. Her thoughts kept returning to the book Jane had given her.

Is that what you are now? she asked herself. *A witch alone?* Once that prospect might have appealed to her. It did have a sort of rebel quality to it, conjuring up images of some wild woman living in her little house in the forest, going out to gather the ingredients for her spells and keeping curiosity seekers away with the stories of her powers. But that was the kind of witch who inhabited fairy tales, not the kind of witch Cooper knew was the reality of being a Wiccan. Real witches were concerned with creating change, not scaring people off. They used magic to learn about the world and to make it a better place. Sure, she could do that on her own if she had to.

And it does look like you'll have to, she thought unhappily. If she wasn't going to be part of any of the local covens, she would have to go it alone. Because she wasn't giving up witchcraft. That much she was sure of. It was too much a part of her, too much in her blood. Her grandmother had been a witch, and even if Cooper's mother had rejected her powers, Cooper had embraced hers. She knew that she had a strong connection to the Goddess and to magic. *And whether anyone else thinks I am or not, I am a witch*, she told herself.

Thinking about her grandmother put another thought in her head. Who had initiated *her*? Had she been part of a coven? Cooper had never really thought about that before. She knew that her grandmother had tried to teach her magic when she was a little girl, and that her mother had asked her not to, but other than that she knew very little about her grandmother's life as a witch, if she had even considered herself a witch at all.

But she must have learned from someone, she told herself. Her grandmother had come from Scotland, and Cooper had always assumed that she had learned what she knew of magic from someone there. But who was it? Was it from *her* own mother or grandmother? Or was it from someone else? It had never really been important to Cooper to know before, but now it was.

Cooper knew from her reading that Scotland had a rich tradition of folk magic, much of which had remained alive even after the dawn of Christianity. Perhaps her grandmother had simply been following the old traditions practiced by many of the people in the Scottish countryside. But maybe it had been more than that. Cooper suspected it was. Something about the way her grandmother had taught her the simple spells she had passed along had seemed more than just the casual passing along of traditions. It was as if she had wanted Cooper to have the knowledge, wanted to awaken something in her.

For the first time since she had been contacted by the ghost of Elizabeth Sanger, Cooper wished she could speak with the dead at will. She would love to talk to her grandmother and hear her story. There were so many questions filling her mind, so much she wanted to know. It would be so easy if she could just call up her grandmother's spirit and get the story from her.

But she couldn't do that. Although she knew that it *was* possible to receive messages from the dead, and although she had on occasion reached the spirits of those who had moved beyond the veil, she knew it wasn't something as easy as picking up the telephone and dialing a number. She could certainly open herself to hearing from her grandmother, but she couldn't be certain that she would be able to reach her.

There was, however, someone she *could* reach. She could talk to her mother. The few times they had discussed Cooper's grandmother, Mrs. Rivers had been either angry or defensive. *But that was quite a while ago*, Cooper reminded herself. *That was when you had so much trouble because of the newspaper articles— the articles written by Amanda Barclay.* Thinking about the newspaper stories that had earned her so much unwanted attention, and that had raised the issues Cooper's mother had with witchcraft, Cooper was reminded once more of Amanda Barclay. *She always seems to be causing me trouble*, she thought, reminded of her father and feeling a stab of pain.

Then she brushed her worries about her father and Amanda Barclay aside. That wasn't her primary concern right now. And her mother didn't know about Cooper's father and Amanda Barclay. Perhaps, Cooper thought, she had forgotten about all of that. After all, they had grown closer in recent months, maybe close enough that Cooper could risk asking some questions about her grandmother.

You have nothing to lose, Cooper told herself as she pulled up outside her house and turned off the car. She looked at the house. The lights were on in the living room. Her mother was home. She could just walk right in and talk to her. But would her mother really know anything? Mrs. Rivers had been so opposed to her mother's magical abilities as a young girl that she had completely shut herself off from ever using her own powers. If she'd been so determined to distance herself from witchcraft, maybe she really didn't know anything about her mother's past.

"There's only one way to find out," Cooper said out loud as she opened her car door and got out.

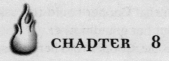

CHAPTER 8

"I have to go," Annie said. "I'm going to be late."

"Okay," replied Juliet. "I'll see you on Saturday."

"I can't wait!" Annie told her.

She hung up the phone and grabbed her coat, heading downstairs as quickly as she could. Her aunt was in the kitchen, looking dazed.

"Are you all right?" Annie asked her.

"Flowers," her aunt answered dully. "Appetizers." She looked at Annie with a shell-shocked expression. "Music."

Annie went and put her arm around her aunt. "It's all going to be fine," she told her. "Everything is under control. We're all going to help. All you have to do is look pretty."

"Dress," Aunt Sarah said.

"It's all being taken care of," Annie said. "I just got off the phone with Juliet. She's coming on Saturday. She'll be here all week. The costumes are coming along fine. Don't worry."

Her aunt sank wearily into a chair and rested her

head in her hands. "I had no idea getting married was so exhausting. No wonder your parents eloped."

"They did?" said Annie, surprised. "I guess that's why I never saw any wedding photos, then."

Aunt Sarah nodded. "They were going to have a real wedding," she said. "But your grandmothers were making them crazy. Your mother's mother wanted a big wedding, and my mother wanted it to be small. They fought like cats and dogs about it. Finally, Peter and Chloe went away for a weekend and when they came back they were married. Now I know why. Your grandmothers were furious, but there was nothing they could do about it."

Annie laughed. "Well, don't get any ideas about running off with Grayson," she told her aunt firmly. "We'll track you down."

She left her aunt in the kitchen with a cup of tea and went out of the house, walking to the bus stop. When she arrived she found Kate waiting.

"Sorry I'm a little late," Annie apologized. "First I was talking to Juliet and then I had to talk Aunt Sarah down. She's freaking."

"I'm not surprised," Kate remarked. "After all, she *is* getting married soon. It's the first time, right?"

Annie nodded.

"I'd be freaked, too," Kate said thoughtfully. "She's been single her whole life."

Annie thought about Kate's remark. Strange as it seemed to her now, she had never really thought of her aunt as being a single woman. But it was true. In all the years that Annie and Meg had lived with her, Aunt Sarah had rarely dated. There had been a handful of men in her life, but none stayed around very long. Annie had never considered the reasons for that, probably because until recently she herself hadn't been particularly interested in guys and romance.

"I guess things really are going to change for her," Annie said to Kate.

"Totally," Kate said. "She's going to be sharing everything from now on. Her closet space. Her bathroom. Her time. She's not a single woman anymore."

"You make it sound so awful," said Annie, suddenly feeling bad for her aunt.

"Personally, I think it sort of would be awful," Kate answered. "Even dating gets kind of claustrophobic, don't you think?"

"I wouldn't know," Annie said. "The only boyfriend I had didn't stick around very long, remember?"

"Sorry," said Kate. "I forgot about that."

"So did I, mostly," Annie said. "I don't really remember what it's like to have a boyfriend."

"Don't pay any attention to me," Kate told her friend. "I'm feeling particularly anti-guy right now."

"Any special reason?" inquired Annie.

"Not really," said Kate as the bus appeared and

pulled to a stop in front of them. When the doors opened two guys their age got off. As they passed the girls they looked at them approvingly.

"Hey," one of them said, smiling.

Kate sighed and rolled her eyes. "That's why," she told Annie as the two of them got on the bus.

"You're tired of guys because they say hi to you?" Annie asked, confused, as they took their seats.

"No," Kate said. "Not just that. It's that they always manage to cause trouble. You think they're all sweet and nice and whatever—and some of them are. But pretty soon you're turning your life upside down for them. You wait for them to call. You try to make yourself look good for them. You go on bad dates to movies *they* like. Why? Because you want them to like you."

"Have you been reading *Cosmo Girl* again?" Annie asked her.

"I've just been doing some thinking," Kate answered. "I want to *do* something with my life. Look at my Aunt Netty. She's going around the world taking these cool photographs and putting a book together. My mom runs her own business. Your aunt has her own business, too. And what have I spent most of my life doing? Trying to get guys to like me."

"That's not true!" objected Annie. "You've done way more than that. You play basketball. You study Wicca. You do a lot of things."

"And why did I start studying Wicca?" Kate

asked. "To get Scott Coogan to go out with me. And why did I stay in Wicca? Because I wanted Tyler to like me."

"That's not why you stayed," Annie said vehemently. "It might have been one of the reasons at first, but it wasn't the real reason." She turned to look at her friend. "Is this about Tyler?" she asked.

Kate didn't say anything for a minute. Then she sighed. "Maybe a little," she admitted.

"You mean maybe a lot," said Annie.

"I know it isn't fair to say this," said Kate. "But I'm mad at him. I feel like once again some guy is taking something I want to be really excited about and making it hard to do that."

"Why is he making it hard?" pressed Annie. "Do you really want to join the Coven of the Green Wood? Is that it?"

"No," answered Kate. "I mean, I don't know. Maybe I would. It's just that I don't like that he's a factor in my decision."

Annie didn't say anything for a moment. For one thing, she wasn't sure what to say. For another, she couldn't help but feel a little bit responsible for Kate's situation. After all, if she hadn't gotten close to Tyler, he might never have broken things off with Kate in the first place. Although Kate had told her time and again that that wasn't true, it still crept into Annie's thoughts at moments like this one.

"Do you remember when Ben Rowe died?" she asked Kate, referring to an old man Annie had befriended while working at a nursing home the year before. He and Annie had become very close, and then he had died unexpectedly.

Kate nodded. "Yes," she said. "It was really hard for you."

"Right," Annie said. "I was really angry at him for dying, and at myself for getting close to him. I thought that if I had just kept my distance it wouldn't have hurt so much when he died. But I was wrong. You don't learn anything from your life by wishing certain things hadn't happened. Even the hard things can be really wonderful."

"I don't wish Tyler hadn't happened," said Kate. "What I wish is that I could stop letting other people become more important to me than I am to me. I'm just not sure how to do that."

"Well," Annie said carefully, "I think you could start by choosing the coven you want to be in based on what *you* want instead of what other people might want. If you worry about what someone else might think, you're not going to choose the right one anyway."

Kate was silent, looking out the window as the bus pulled to their stop in town. As the girls got up to leave she said, "This would be a lot easier if they just assigned you to a coven, like it was your home-room or something."

They walked to the bookstore and went inside, where the rest of the class was already gathered in the back room. Annie and Kate said their hellos and then settled onto their cushions to wait for class to begin. A few minutes later Sophia came in.

"Merry meet," she said cheerfully. "We have quite a bit to do tonight, so I'm just going to launch into it. Tonight you're going to hear from two coven representatives. One will be familiar to you, while the other will not. We'll start with the one you know."

Annie was pleased to see Thatcher Morris walk to the front of the room. Thatcher was one of the older members of the Coven of the Green Wood. A carpenter, he had a long gray beard and sparkling, mischievous eyes. Annie always thought of him as a kind of Wiccan Santa Claus, an image that was made even more real when Thatcher broke into his unmistakable deep laugh.

"Greetings," Thatcher said merrily. "As all of you know, I'm one of the members of the Coven of the Green Wood. So are many of the teachers you've had throughout this past year. And that's no coincidence. The Coven of the Green Wood was designed as a teaching coven. In other words, we prepare people to go out and teach Wicca to others. Our members are frequently asked to participate in classes such as this one. We also teach at numerous weekend and week-long retreats. Some of us have also been known to teach the odd course or two at Jasper College and other local institutes of higher learning. And I *do* mean the odd course," he emphasized, laughing at his own joke.

Annie laughed along with Thatcher. She hadn't realized that the Coven of the Green Wood had an emphasis on preparing teachers. Now that she knew that, she was intrigued. How did it work? What did the coven do? She raised her hand.

"What exactly does a teaching coven do?" she asked.

"Teach," Thatcher answered with a deadpan expression. Then his face broke into a broad smile. "Just teasing. We are similar to the Daughters of the Cauldron in that we are an eclectic coven," Thatcher said. "We think it's important for those teaching Wicca to others to have a broad working knowledge of how other traditions function. So we draw from a variety of sources for our rituals. But the most important aspect of our coven's work is that more experienced members share their experiences and their teaching methods with less experienced members. And I'm not talking about older and younger, necessarily. Some of our younger members are more experienced than some of our older ones. Everyone works together, and over the years we've designed a training course that prepares our members to teach others what Wicca is and how it can change their lives."

"Do you have to have teaching experience to join?" asked Emma.

Thatcher shook his head. "No," he said. "But you do have to want to teach, and you have to have some aptitude for sharing Wicca with others." He looked at the seven initiates seated before him. "Teaching is definitely *not* for everyone," he said. "And there's nothing wrong with not wanting to teach. We all have our individual skills in Wicca. But if you do think that you'd like to eventually teach witchcraft to others, the Coven of the Green Wood might be a good place for you."

There were no additional questions for Thatcher, so he thanked everyone for listening and moved to the back of the room. Then Sophia returned.

"You've now heard from the two covens you've spent the most time with," she said. "But you've also been in rituals with members of other covens, particularly at the Midsummer and Yule rituals that some of you attended. One of those covens is run by my friend Polly. She's now going to tell you something about her coven."

A tall, heavyset woman with long blond hair came forward. She and Sophia embraced, and then Polly turned and looked at the class. She had soft blue eyes, and when she spoke her voice was quiet.

"My coven is called Freya's Circle," she said. "As you might be able to tell from the name, we're a coven whose primary interest is in the Norse gods and goddesses. We love ritual, and we design our sabbats around the legends of Norse mythology. We also study the shamanistic practices of the Norse peoples, and we spend quite a bit of time working with drumming, runes, and meditation. We're pretty evenly mixed between men and women, and although we consider Freya to be the principal deity of our coven we also work quite a bit with the gods Odin and Balder."

"Better watch out," Kate whispered to Annie. "Remember what happened last time you played around with Freya."

Annie had been thinking the exact same thing. When she had invoked the Norse goddess during a full moon ritual, her life had been turned upside down. She tried to imagine what it would be like being in a coven where the feisty goddess was invoked on a regular basis. *It might be a lot of fun*, she thought.

"Do you celebrate the same eight sabbats as other witches?" Ezra asked Polly.

Polly nodded. "Yes, we do," she said. "We also add several important days from the Norse calendar, particularly the birthdays of Freya and some of the other deities."

"And what about being part of a larger clan?" Laura inquired. "I know some of the people who practice the Norse religion are very into the idea of clans and kinship."

"Many are," Polly said. "The Norse religion, also called Asatru, was very much based on the concept of clans and brotherhood. We've moved away from that. Our coven does work with other covens, like when we took part in the Midsummer and Midwinter rituals. But we don't belong to a larger network of Norse covens. We formed primarily because a lot of us related to the Norse legends and found them to be wonderful ways to express our own spirituality."

Laura nodded, her question answered. When no one else had questions for Polly, she smiled and joined Thatcher in the back, letting Sophia take over once more.

"So tonight you heard about two very different types of covens," Sophia told the class. "Remember, no one is asking you to decide right now what you think might be right for you. We're just presenting you with information. Next week we'll hear from two more covens. That will be it. The week after, all the representatives will be here and you will all be asked to make your choices. But for tonight we're done. If you want to talk to Polly and Thatcher, they'll be around."

After helping put the room back together, Annie went to speak to Polly. No one else had approached her, and she was standing shyly to one side. When Annie came up to her, she smiled.

"I was starting to feel like the girl no one asks to dance," she said.

Annie laughed. "Been there," she said.

"Are you interested in Norse magic?" Polly inquired.

Annie shook her head. "I really don't know all that much about it," she said. "I read up on Asatru for an assignment we had in class, and I did some work with Freya. It didn't exactly turn out the way I thought it would," she added.

Polly smiled. "She can be a tricky one sometimes," she said.

"Tell me about it," said Annie. "I still have the miniskirt to prove it."

Polly raised her eyebrow in a questioning look.

"Long story," Annie said. "What I really wanted to ask you about was how the coven is set up. Do you have a high priestess or what?"

"We have a priest and a priestess," Polly answered. "I'm the high priestess. My husband, Bern, is the high priest. We run the coven together. We're a little more formal than the Coven of the Green Wood or the Daughters of the Cauldron. But we're not *too* rigid. We do like creativity in our members."

"But you stick to the Norse deities," said Annie.

"Right," Polly answered. "We find that it strengthens our circle and makes it easier to raise and focus energy when we concentrate on one or two main deities."

"Okay," Annie said. "That's really what I wanted to ask. Thanks."

"It's my pleasure," said Polly. "I hope you'll consider joining us."

Annie smiled and walked over to Kate, who had just finished talking to Thatcher.

"Well?" Kate asked. "Will you be donning reindeer robes and learning runes?"

"I doubt it," said Annie. "I like all the Norse stuff, but I don't think it's quite what I'm looking for. How about you? Did Thatcher make you feel any better about joining the Coven of the Green Wood?"

"Hard to say," replied Kate. "I kind of like the idea of the teaching focus. I know it's not really like me, but something about it is appealing. Like I said earlier, I want to *do* something with myself. That might be a good path to take."

"What about Tyler?" inquired Annie.

"That's still an issue," Kate told her. "I really have to think about it some more."

"Well, we have two weeks to decide," Annie told her.

Kate looked at her. "This isn't easy, is it?" she said.

Annie smiled. "No," she said. "But like I told you, sometimes the most rewarding things are the hardest."

CHAPTER 9

"You did what?" Cooper asked Kate the next morning as they stood at their lockers.

"I asked Tyler to go out with me tonight," said Kate, looking slightly embarrassed.

"Why?" asked Sasha, who was leaning up against the lockers.

"Yeah," Annie echoed. "Why?"

Kate clutched her books to her chest. "I think we need to talk some things out," she answered.

"I thought all you guys did was talk things out," remarked Sasha. "Not that that's bad or anything," she added when Kate shot her an annoyed look.

"Yes," Kate said. "We *have* talked a lot. But there's just some stuff I need to say to him, so I asked him to get something to eat tonight."

"Want us to come?" Cooper asked. "We can hide in a booth nearby and pretend we just happened to be there. That way, if you need to ditch him you have an out."

"Thanks, but no," said Kate. "I'm going to be very adult about this."

The bell rang and the four of them scattered to their respective classes. Kate and Sasha both had English, so they walked together.

"Are you talking to Tyler because you're thinking of joining the Coven of the Green Wood?" asked Sasha.

"Partly," Kate answered. "But mostly it's for me. Before I decide which coven I want to be part of, I want to say good-bye to some parts of myself."

Sasha nodded. "Letting go of the past," she said. "Good plan. You should do a ritual around that."

Kate looked at her. "You know, that's not a bad idea," she said. "I might just do that."

"And to think that you guys are the ones being initiated and I'm just a lowly dedicant," Sasha said dramatically.

"Give me a break," Kate said, laughing. "This time next year you'll be making the same decision. Then we'll see how easy you think it is."

"You need one of those Sorting Hats, like in the Harry Potter books," Sasha suggested. "Then it could make the decisions for you."

"You've been reading Harry Potter?" Kate asked, surprised.

"Hey, inside this tough girl is a little kid," said Sasha as they entered their classroom. "Besides, who can resist a guy with a scar?"

* * *

Later that day, while she was getting ready to go meet Tyler, Kate thought about what Sasha had said. Although she hadn't wanted to admit it, she too had read the Harry Potter books. *Sasha was right*, she thought as she got dressed. *This would all be a lot easier if the Sorting Hat just assigned us to covens*. But she knew that it was important for a witch to choose her own coven, not join one based on what someone else thought.

"I guess I'll just have to do it the old-fashioned way," she told her reflection in the mirror.

She finished getting ready and then took the bus downtown. She had asked Tyler to meet her at a sandwich shop. She hadn't wanted to go to the hamburger place they'd used to go to when they were together, and she didn't want to meet him somewhere fancy, in case he thought that maybe they were on a date. The sandwich shop was a neutral choice, not romantic and not fancy. *We'll just get a sandwich, I'll say what I have to say, and I'll leave*, Kate thought as she entered the restaurant.

Tyler was already there, seated at a booth in the back. When Kate joined him he smiled at her. "Hey," he said. "It's good to see you."

"Thanks," Kate said, deliberately not adding that it was good to see him, too. She picked up the menu handed to her by the waitress and opened it. Looking at the list of offerings allowed her to not look at Tyler.

Tyler lasted about a minute and a half before

asking, "So, why did you ask me to meet you tonight?"

Well, he sure gets to the point, thought Kate. She closed her menu and laid it down.

"I wanted to tell you that I'm considering joining the Coven of the Green Wood," she said.

Tyler's face lit up. "That's great," he said.

"But not because you're in it," Kate added quickly.

Tyler's face fell. "Well, no," he said. "I didn't think that was why."

"I like the idea of learning how to teach," Kate told him, trying to keep her voice calm and neutral. "I think that might be good for me."

Tyler nodded but didn't say anything.

"What?" Kate said, seeing the look on his face. "You don't think I'd make a good teacher?"

"I hadn't really thought about it before," Tyler answered.

"But now that you're thinking about it, you don't think I would, do you?" Kate demanded.

Tyler looked uncomfortable. "I think you could learn a lot from being in the coven," he said. "And not everyone ends up teaching the way Thatcher does."

"Oh," Kate said. "So what you're saying is that you think I couldn't do what *you* do. I see."

"Kate," Tyler said, "I didn't say that."

"No, but it's what you were thinking," Kate retorted.

Tyler put up his hands. "Whatever you say," he said.

"Don't you dare whatever me," snapped Kate. She was getting angry now, and she felt her temper flaring up. "Admit it—you don't think I'd make a good teacher."

"I told you, I think the coven would be a good place for you."

"Why?" asked Kate. "So you can keep an eye on me? So you can feel like I've forgiven you for cheating on me with my best friend?" She hadn't meant to make that last remark, but it had slipped out.

Tyler looked away. "I thought we were past that," he said.

"I'm sorry," Kate said. "You're right. That wasn't fair."

Tyler looked at her. "Kate, I'd like you in the coven because I think we could work well together."

"You're still avoiding the whole teacher issue," Kate said testily.

"Okay," Tyler said. "Maybe I've never really thought of you as the teacher type."

Kate bit her lip. Thinking that Tyler didn't see her as teacher material had been difficult enough; hearing him actually say it hurt more than she cared to admit.

"I didn't mean to hurt your feelings," Tyler said when she didn't reply to him.

Kate gave a little laugh. "No," she said. "You never do."

She looked across the table. Once she had

thought that Tyler was the most considerate, thoughtful guy she'd ever met. Now she couldn't even look at him.

"I have to go," she said, sliding out of the booth.

"What?" Tyler said, surprised. "Where are you going?"

"Away from you," said Kate as she walked away from him.

She exited the restaurant and began walking toward the bus stop. Moments later she heard Tyler running down the sidewalk after her.

"Kate!" he called out. "Wait."

She didn't wait. She kept walking. But Tyler was running, and he quickly caught up with her.

"Hey," he said. "Can't we talk?"

"Apparently not," said Kate, facing him and looking him in the eye.

"How did this get so ugly?" Tyler asked her. "What happened?"

"I let myself think that you're something you're not," Kate said flatly.

"Which is what?" said Tyler.

"I thought you were different," said Kate. "I thought you really wanted me to be the best person I could be—the best witch I could be. But you don't. You want me in your coven, but not because you think I'd be a good addition to it. You want me there so you can make sure I don't get *too* good."

"That is so not true!" Tyler said angrily.

"Isn't it?" asked Kate. "I think it is. I think

you're just like all the other guys out there. You like a girl until she proves she's her own person." She regarded Tyler for a moment. "Scott was the same way," she said.

"Don't even mention me in the same sentence as that guy," Tyler said. "I don't know what's gotten into you, but you've got things all wrong. I *do* want you to be the best witch you can be, Kate. And I do think you'd be a great addition to the coven. All right, so maybe I've never thought of you as being a teacher, but maybe I'm wrong. Prove me wrong. Join the Coven of the Green Wood and show me what you can do."

The two of them stood on the sidewalk, staring at one another but not speaking. Kate was still furiously angry. Her heart was thumping in her chest, and she could feel her hands shaking. She knew that Tyler was challenging her, and she knew that the only way she was going to prove her point to him was by accepting it.

"Fine," she said. "I will."

With that she turned and walked away from him.

"Good," he said. "You do that."

Kate half expected Tyler to chase after her again, but she didn't hear the sound of his shoes behind her, and when she turned around after walking half a block he was nowhere in sight.

"I still won," she said out loud. Then she turned and practically skipped back to the bus stop.

When she got home she found her father in the

kitchen, getting something to eat. He was staring into the refrigerator with a lost expression.

"What is all this stuff?" he asked Kate as she came into the room.

Kate peered over his shoulder. "That stuff in the blue bowl is lobster salad," she said. "The thing in the Tupperware is a roast chicken. I'm not sure what's in that container, but it's either vegetarian lasagna or mushroom ravioli."

"I'll go for the lobster salad," her father said, taking the blue bowl out of the refrigerator. He sat down at the table, took the plastic wrap off the bowl, and stuck a fork into the salad.

"Don't you want a plate?" Kate asked. "Mom would kill you if she knew you were eating straight out of the bowl."

"Your mother's not here," her father said, as if that justified everything. He went to the refrigerator and returned with a bottle of beer.

"Good point," said Kate. She got a fork and sat across from her father, spearing a piece of lobster and popping it into her mouth.

"I thought you were going out with your friends," her father said, opening his beer and taking a drink.

"Just one friend," Kate told him. "Tyler. But we cut it short."

Her father looked at her quizzically. "Going out with Tyler again?" he asked.

Kate snorted. "Not in this lifetime," she said.

"No offense, but your kind are not exactly high on my list of favorite things right now."

"My kind," her father said. "What did we do now?" His voice suggested that more than once he'd been required to defend the entire male species from attacks by women.

"What is it with you guys?" asked Kate, getting herself a soda from the refrigerator and taking out the chicken while she was at it. "Why do you always have to be in charge?"

Her father laughed, almost choking on his beer. "Us?" he said. "You think *we're* in charge? If your mother heard that she'd have something to say about it."

"Come on," Kate argued. "Why is it that whenever a woman starts being independent and strong, guys flip out on us?"

"Did Tyler flip out on you?" her father asked.

"Well, no, not exactly," admitted Kate as she poked at the chicken and pulled a strip of crispy skin off. "But he told me he didn't think I'd make a good teacher."

"You want to be a teacher?" said her father.

"Not as in a career," explained Kate. "At least, I don't think I do. This is about joining his coven."

Her father looked down, and Kate realized what she'd said. She and her father never really talked about the fact that she was being initiated as a witch. He had tried his best to talk her out of it, even asking her to speak with the family priest before making her decision. He had agreed to stand by her choice if she agreed to do that, and he had. But Kate knew he wasn't happy about it, and she did her best not to upset him by talking too much about her Wiccan activities.

"We don't have to talk about this if you don't want to," she said quietly.

Her father held up his hand. "No," he said. "We should. So you want to join this—group—that Tyler is part of."

He can't even say the word coven, Kate thought. *But at least he's trying.*

"It's one of my choices, yes," Kate said. "And Tyler said he was okay with me doing that. But tonight he basically told me he didn't think I was smart enough to teach other people about . . . about the Craft," she said, choosing to use the name for witchcraft that sounded the least witchy.

"Of course you're smart enough," her father said instantly. "You can do anything you want to."

"That's what I told Tyler," said Kate. "Well, after I told him what a jerk he was."

Her father laughed. "Let me guess, and then you ran out of the restaurant."

"I did not *run*," Kate said defensively. "I walked quickly."

Her father laughed again. "You're just like your mother," he said.

"What do you mean?" Kate asked him.

"One time, when we had been dating about six

months, your mother and I went skiing," her father told her. "She wanted to go down this difficult hill. I made the mistake of telling her that maybe she should stick to something easier. Well, you can imagine what she did."

"She went down the hill," Kate said, knowing that she would do the same thing.

Her father nodded. "About halfway down she fell. She rolled the rest of the way down."

"Was she hurt?" Kate asked.

Her father shook his head. "Just a little bruised," he said. "But I'll never forget what she said when I met her at the bottom. She looked at me and she said, 'I wouldn't have fallen if you hadn't made me so angry.'"

Kate laughed. "That sounds like Mom," she said.

"So, did you fall halfway down?" her father asked her.

"What do you mean?" Kate asked him.

"I mean, did you do something just to prove to Tyler that he was wrong, something you maybe wish you hadn't?"

"I agreed to join his co—his group," said Kate, using her father's choice of words.

"And is that what you really want?" asked Mr. Morgan.

"Yes," Kate said.

Her father didn't say anything in response, concentrating on finding a big lump of lobster meat in the salad.

"What?" Kate said, knowing that there was

something he wasn't saying.

"Nothing," her father replied. "You said yes."

"And I meant yes," said Kate.

"Okay," said her father.

"You don't believe me," Kate said.

"I don't have to believe you," said Mr. Morgan simply. "You have to believe you."

"You're as bad as he is!" Kate said. "I swear, you guys have some kind of pact to always stick up for each other."

"I'm not sticking up for anyone," her father said. "I'm just saying."

Kate took a bite of chicken and chewed it, watching her father. She knew he was up to something. He was behaving the same way he behaved whenever he and her mother got into an argument.

"I do want to be in the Coven of the Green Wood," she said finally.

Her father shrugged. "It's up to you," he said.

"I do," Kate said again. *I do*, she thought to herself as her father attacked the lobster salad once more. *I really do*. She looked at the chicken. *At least I'm pretty sure I do*, she thought.

CHAPTER 10

"That's Betty Bangs," Cooper said excitedly.

"Where?" asked Annie. She, Cooper, and Sasha had just walked into Black Eyed Susan's. It was Friday night, and the place was filled with people who had come to hear the battle of the bands.

"Over there," said Cooper. "The one in the Blondie T-shirt and leather pants."

"She looks cool," Sasha said appreciatively.

"She is cool," Cooper said. "Scrapple is one of the best bands around." She looked around the club. "I wonder where Jane is?"

A moment later Jane materialized, coming in the front door.

"She has someone with her," Annie remarked as Jane made her way over to them, using her guitar case to push people out of the way as a girl followed along behind her.

"That must be Siobhan," Cooper said happily. When Jane reached them Cooper hugged her and whispered in her ear, "She's so cute."

"Everyone, this is Siobhan," Jane said.

The girls all introduced themselves. Siobhan shook hands and smiled. Cooper pointed out Betty Bangs to Jane.

"I hope she likes our cover of 'Song for a Tired Girl,'" Jane said. The two of them had rehearsed for several hours the night before, with the Scrapple song one of the tunes they'd spent the most time on.

"I do, too," said Cooper. She looked at her friends. "We have to get backstage," she said. "Do you guys mind?"

"No," said Sasha. "We'll wait for Kate. Besides, we have to grill Siobhan, and it's easier if you're not here."

Jane looked at her friend. "Don't worry," she said. "They're harmless."

"We'll be standing right up front when you guys play," Annie assured them.

Cooper and Jane left the three of them in the club and headed backstage. There they found lots of women hanging around, tuning their instruments and warming up their throats.

"This is so cool," Cooper said as she and Jane found a place to unpack their guitars. "I've never seen so many rocker girls in one place. It's like Ozzfest and Lilith Fair got all jumbled together."

"You don't think they're giving Siobhan a hard time, do you?" Jane asked, sounding preoccupied.

"She'll be fine," said Cooper. She watched Jane put her guitar strap around her neck and start to play with the tuning pegs. "She seems nice," she said.

Jane blushed. "It's just that, you know, this is the first time I've introduced anyone to my friends."

"They'll be nice to her," Cooper assured her. "If they're not I'll beat them up myself."

"Okay, ladies."

Cooper turned and saw a woman standing in the midst of all the musicians. She had a clipboard in her hand, and she was holding it up for everyone to see.

"This is the roster for tonight," she said. "Batcave will go first, followed by Cindy's Notebook. Lemon Fizz will be third, and then we'll have the Bitter Pills before winding it all up with Messy Lucy. You'll each get a fifteen-minute set, and you can do however many songs you can fit into that time period. Any questions?"

"When do we get to meet Betty Bangs?" called out a girl who was practicing her drum licks on the wall as she spoke.

The woman with the clipboard waited until the catcalls that followed the girl's question settled down. "Betty is a very busy lady," she said. "She'll present the prize to the winners. Whether she stays around afterward or not is up to her."

"What is the prize?" Jane asked. While a prize had been mentioned on the flyer, what it was hadn't been specified.

"That's a surprise," said the woman. "But trust me—the winners will be more than satisfied."

Murmurs filled the air as everyone talked about

what the prize might be. The woman with the clip-board waved for their attention again. "I'm going to go start the show," she said. "Be ready when you're called or I'll have to cut you."

She slipped through the curtains to the stage, and Cooper heard the people in the audience clap.

"Welcome to Black Eyed Susan's," the woman said, her voice amplified by the club's sound system.

"Do you think we'll win?" Jane asked Cooper.

Cooper shrugged. "Why not?" she said. "We won the last time we played, right?"

Jane nodded.

"Then why not this time?" said Cooper. "I mean, really, do you think we're going to lose to someone called Lemon Fizz?"

Jane laughed as a girl near them shot them a look. Cooper put her hand over her mouth and pre-tended to be embarrassed. "Guess she's with the band," she whispered to Jane, making her laugh.

"It would be so cool to win in front of Siobhan," said Jane.

Cooper grinned. "Well, I'll do my best to help you score big points," she said.

The woman onstage was announcing the judges. Cooper heard her mention a local music critic, as well as the owner of the record store where Jane had found the flyer. Then the woman said, "And visiting us from Seattle, where her band, Scrapple, revolutionized the rock world, is none other than Betty Bangs."

The club erupted in applause, as did the back-stage area. Cooper knew that every girl in the place probably was there because of Betty Bangs, and she really wanted to impress Betty with the way she and Jane played. Having one of her idols hear *her* play was a dream come true.

"And now let's get the evening started with four girls who spent *way* too much time reading comic books when they were little," the announcer said. "Give it up for Batcave."

The members of Batcave went onstage. A moment later Cooper heard their drummer count down the intro and the band launched into its first song.

"They're good," Jane said after listening for a minute or two.

"They're okay," Cooper said. "They sound too much like a Runaways rip-off."

Batcave played four songs before their time was up, after which the audience applauded and the announcer came back on. "Okay," she said. "While the judges think about that performance, we'll let the next band get ready."

The girls from Batcave came backstage as the three members of Cindy's Notebook took their places.

"Good job," Cooper said to the guitarist from Batcave, who was standing near her.

"Thanks," the girl said. "I think we did okay."

"I don't know if Betty did," the bassist said.

"She barely looked at us."

Cooper looked at Jane. The whole reason she was there was because of Betty Bangs. If Betty didn't like her music, she didn't know what she would do.

Cooper listened as Cindy's Notebook began their set. But her mind wasn't on their music. She was thinking about how awful it would be if Betty Bangs ignored her—or, worse, gave her a lousy score.

"I feel sick," she said to Jane.

"What?" Jane said. "You never feel sick before we play. I'm the one who's supposed to feel sick."

"Well, I do," Cooper said, leaning against the wall.

"You'll be fine," Jane assured her. "Besides, we're almost on. There's just one more band to go."

The girls from Lemon Fizz were readying themselves to go onstage. The singer gave Cooper a withering look as she walked past, and Cooper groaned.

"She's probably Betty Bangs's best friend," she said to Jane. "They've probably known each other since they were five."

"Will you get over it?" Jane said. "We're going to be great."

Cooper didn't say anything. She slumped miserably against the wall, listening to Lemon Fizz start their first song. She hated to admit it, but they were good. Although she wanted to block them out and focus on getting ready for her own set, she couldn't help but listen. The band played through two songs. Then the singer said, "Lemon Fizz owes a lot to groups like Scrapple. In honor of Betty, we'd like to do our favorite Scrapple song."

Jane and Cooper exchanged glances. "They're not," Jane said as the familiar guitar opening of "Song for a Tired Girl" ripped through the club.

"They are," Cooper said, closing her eyes. How could this be happening? *That was supposed to be our big surprise*, she thought.

"Okay," Jane said. "We have to come up with something else. We can't do the same song. What else can we do? How about that one you've been working on? You know, 'Rain on My Face' or 'Rain on the Roof,' or whatever it is."

"It's 'Rain on My Parade,'" Cooper said. "And no, we're not doing that. We have to do a Scrapple song."

"But they took ours!" Jane wailed.

"We know other ones," said Cooper. "Just think."

Lemon Fizz was finishing up the song. The Bitter Pills were on next. "We have, like, thirty seconds," Cooper told Jane.

The Lemon Fizz girls finished their set and left the stage to thunderous applause. "We're on," Cooper said.

"But what song are we doing?" Jane asked.

"I'll tell you when it's time," said Cooper, taking her friend's hand and dragging her along.

She and Jane passed through the curtain and walked onto the stage as the announcer was saying, "It's time to take your Bitter Pills, ladies and gentlemen."

As she and Jane plugged their guitars into the amplifiers, Cooper looked out at the audience. There, standing right at the edge of the stage, were her friends. And off to the side was the judges' table. Cooper glanced over and saw Betty Bangs looking down at the paper in front of her. *She's not even looking at us*, Cooper thought.

But there was no time to dwell on it. It was time to play. Cooper looked at Jane, who nodded. Without saying a word to the audience, Cooper began playing. Their first song was a wild, rough number called "None for You." Jane had written it, and she sang lead. Cooper concentrated on playing her guitar, joining in on the chorus. When the song was over, the audience clapped appreciatively.

Just keep focused on the music, Cooper told herself, fighting the temptation to see if Betty Bangs was watching them. Instead she started on the next song, which was one she'd written titled "When I Sleep." It was a new song, and she really liked it. She and Jane had never played it live before, and Cooper was glad to see people singing along after hearing the first chorus. It made her feel less worried about the judges, particularly Betty, and she found herself loosening up. By the third number, a collaboration between her and Jane called "Fill It Up With Regular," she was enjoying herself.

Then it was time for the last song. As the audience's applause died down, Cooper saw Jane watching her expectantly. She had to decide, and quickly, whether they would do one of their own songs or go ahead with a Scrapple tune. Finally, Cooper allowed herself to look over at Betty Bangs. She was still looking at her paper.

I'll give her something that will get her attention, Cooper thought. She leaned over to Jane. "Let's do 'Anything for Attention.'"

Jane looked surprised. "Are you sure?" she asked.

Cooper nodded. The song was one of the more obscure Scrapple songs, but it was one of Jane and Cooper's favorites. They'd only played it a few times together, though, and then only for fun. They'd never seriously practiced it. "Just go for it," Cooper told Jane.

Cooper leaned into her microphone. "Like Lemon Fizz, and probably like most people here, Jane and I are big Scrapple fans," she said. "At the risk of looking like total suck-ups, we'd like to do this last song for Betty. Thanks for making us want to play."

With that she began the song. *Just have fun*, she told herself. *That's what playing rock music is all about*. And she did. She let go and gave everything she had to the song. Jane did the same. Pretty soon Cooper forgot about Betty Bangs, and about the competition, and she remembered how much she loved just being onstage, playing good music with Jane.

When the song came to its end Cooper played the final chord and then reached over to grab Jane's hand, lifting it in triumph. She gave a final wave to her friends, who clapped madly, and then she and Jane went back through the curtain, where the first thing they saw was the singer from Lemon Fizz.

"Nice idea, doing a Scrapple cover," she said, clearly being sarcastic. "Too bad you didn't think of it first."

Cooper ignored her as she and Jane put away their guitars. The last band was on, and Cooper was still enjoying the rush she got from playing live. She barely noticed when Messy Lucy finished and the announcer came back for a final time.

"All right," she said. "It's time to hear who our judges picked as tonight's winner. But before we announce that, let me just say that the prize tonight is a guitar autographed by Miss Betty Bangs herself."

"Oh," Cooper said, gripping Jane's hand. "I *so* want to win that."

There was a pause as someone brought the announcer the results of the judging. Cooper held her breath as the woman took what seemed like hours to read them.

"It looks like tonight's lucky winners are—Lemon Fizz!" she called out finally.

Cooper's heart sank. "Lemon Fizz?" she said to Jane as the members of that group streamed onstage.

Jane looked crestfallen. "I guess you can't win every time," she said.

Cooper picked up her guitar. "Let's get out of here," she said. She wanted to get as far away from the club as she could, before what little high she still had from playing evaporated completely.

She and Jane went out front, where their friends were waiting for them.

"You guys really kicked butt," Kate said.

"Thanks," Cooper said, meaning it.

"I don't know why that other band won," Siobhan said to Jane. "You guys were much better."

"*Loads* better," said someone beside Annie.

Cooper saw a girl standing there, hanging back a bit. She was a little younger than Cooper and her friends, with shoulder-length blond hair and glasses. Seeing Cooper looking at her, she blushed.

"I'm Anne," she said shyly. "Anne Rouyer. I just wanted to tell you that I love the way you play."

"Thanks," said Cooper.

"I saw you guys play once before," Anne said. "At Bar None. You were amazing."

"You mean you came here to see *us*?" Jane asked her.

Anne nodded. "I want to be in a band," she said.

127

"I sing and play guitar a little. Not as good as you guys do," she added.

Jane looked at Cooper, and suddenly losing didn't matter anymore. Cooper couldn't believe that the girl had come to see *her*, the same way she went to see bands that inspired her.

"My favorite song of yours is 'Why Should I Care?'" Anne told Cooper. "I wish I could write something like that."

Cooper wasn't sure what to say to the girl. Anne was her first fan. Well, her first fan besides her friends. Cooper felt like she should say something nice to Anne, but she found herself unable to think of anything.

"Ask her to hang out with you."

Cooper turned and found Betty Bangs standing next to her. She was so shocked she couldn't even react.

"Ask her to hang out with you," Betty whispered in Cooper's ear. "You'll make her night."

"Um, would you like to hang out with us?" Cooper said, turning back to Anne, who seemed totally oblivious to the fact that Betty Bangs was there.

Anne's face lit up. "Could I?" she asked.

"Sure," Cooper said. "Why don't you all go get a table. I'll be there in a minute."

Kate, Annie, and Siobhan took Anne and went to find a table. Jane, having seen Betty, remained behind. When their friends were gone, Betty shook Cooper's hand, then Jane's.

"I just wanted to tell you guys that you really rock," she said.

Cooper was stunned. "But we lost," she said.

Betty snorted. "Not because of me," she said. "I gave you guys first place. It was the two guys who voted for Lemon Fluff or whatever they were called. They thought the singer was hot—and she flirted with them before the show. Typical music business stuff."

"You gave us first place?" Jane said.

Betty nodded. "That cover of 'Anything for Attention' was even better than my original. I loved how you guys gave it that raw, unrehearsed feel."

Jane and Cooper exchanged glances but didn't say anything. Cooper wanted to confess to Betty that their version *had* been raw and unrehearsed, but she was so excited by Betty's compliment that she let it ride. *Better than her original*, Cooper kept repeating to herself.

"These other bands were okay," Betty said, waving her hand dismissively. "But you guys were something different. What are your plans for this summer?"

"I don't know," Cooper said. "I haven't really thought about it."

"Well, think about it," Betty told her. She took a card out of her pocket. "This is my manager. Call her next week. I'm putting together a women-in-rock tour, and I'd be really interested in having you guys play the small stage on the West Coast leg if you're interested."

Cooper stared at the card in her hand. Was Betty joking? Had she really just asked Cooper and Jane to play on a real concert tour?

"Like I said, you guys are originals," Betty told them. "I like people who do their own thing. Keep it up. And call that number. I've got to get out of here, but I'm sure I'll see you two again soon. And don't forget your little groupie. She's waiting for you over there."

All Cooper could do was nod at Betty as she disappeared into the crowd. It took another minute before she could look at Jane and say, "Did that just happen?"

"Uh-huh," said Jane, nodding.

"Betty Bangs just asked us to tour with Scrapple?" Cooper said.

"Uh-huh," said Jane again.

The two girls looked at each other.

"She said we were originals," said Jane. "She said we do our own thing."

Cooper looked again at the card in her hand. *Do our own thing*, she thought. She had always prided herself on not having to be like everyone else, of not having to be part of a group. Suddenly a thought came to her. *You don't just have to be an original when it comes to your music,* she told herself. *You can do it with magic, too.*

Cooper looked at the table where her friends were waiting. She saw Anne Rouyer watching her intently. "Let's go mingle with our adoring public," Cooper said to Jane. *And later,* she thought, *I'm going to present Kate and Annie with a proposition.*

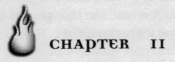

CHAPTER II

"When Becka and her dad move in, this is going to be his office," Annie said as she turned on the light in the room next to Meg's. "But until then it's the guest bedroom."

Juliet looked around at the room. Inspired by Annie's and Becka's paint job, Grayson and Aunt Sarah had decided to tackle the office as well. It had taken most of the previous Sunday to clean the room of the junk that had accumulated there over the years. Some of it had gone down to the basement, some to the garage, and some directly into the trash. Once the room was empty, the walls had been painted a rich chocolate color. Because the room got a lot of light during the day, the newly painted walls gave off a warm glow that wasn't at all dark or depressing. And once Grayson's big oak desk was moved in, the room was going to be beautiful. At the moment it held a bed, a dresser, and an armchair that Annie and her aunt had set up so that Juliet could have her own room during her visit.

"This is great," said Juliet, putting her suitcase on the bed.

"I'll show you my room next," said Annie, taking her sister by the hand and dragging her down the hallway and up the weird little staircase that led to the part of the house where Annie—and now Becka—had their rooms.

"I love it," Juliet exclaimed when she saw Annie's bedroom. "It's so big and airy."

"Isn't it?" said Annie. "In the summer the breeze is fantastic. It smells like the ocean and roses and pine trees."

Juliet was walking around Annie's room, looking at everything. She stopped in front of the large painting hanging opposite Annie's bed—a painting that had been done by their mother. It showed Annie as a baby, being held by Mrs. Crandall as she looked out the window at a full moon. Juliet gazed at the picture for a minute without saying anything, then moved on. She stopped in front of Annie's altar.

"That's a beautiful goddess statue," she said, looking at the image of a large, round woman that was surrounded by small white and green candles on the altar. "What's it made out of?"

"Salt dough," Annie said. "I made it for the Spring Equinox. We used to make Christmas ornaments out of salt dough when I was in second grade. I thought I could probably use it to make a goddess statue. She didn't bake all the way through, but I like her."

Juliet laughed. "Half baked or not, I think she's cool."

Annie was relieved that Juliet didn't think her altar was weird. Although they had talked about Annie's involvement in Wicca, this was the first time Juliet had actually seen any real evidence of her little sister's witchcraft studies. She looked at the things on the altar for another minute or so and then turned around.

"We should go downstairs," she said. "Aunt Sarah has probably already gotten into the costumes."

When they'd picked Juliet up at the airport that afternoon, she had been carrying not only her own suitcase but two huge bags containing the costumes she'd been working on for the wedding. The bags had been deposited in the living room before Annie had shown Juliet to her bedroom. Both Aunt Sarah and Meg had been eyeing them with great interest, and Annie knew they wouldn't be able to hold out for too long.

As she and Juliet went down the stairs to the kitchen, Juliet laughed. "It feels so strange saying Aunt Sarah," she told Annie. "I grew up with an Aunt Shirley, an Aunt Charlene, an Aunt Jean, and an Aunt Edith. I'm so used to saying their names that saying Aunt Sarah makes me feel like I've gotten the names mixed up or something."

"You'll get used to it," Annie told her. "Besides, she's so freaked out about the wedding that she'd probably answer to just about anything."

They walked through the kitchen to the living room, where they found Meg unzipping one of the bags.

"Ah-ha!" Juliet exclaimed, making Meg jump. "Caught you."

Meg turned a guilty face to them. "I was just testing the zipper," she said quickly. "It looked like it might be broken."

"That's true," said Aunt Sarah. "We were just saying that it would be too bad if the zipper was broken and you couldn't use the bag anymore."

"Liars," Juliet said, shaking her head sadly. "I've come to a house of liars." She turned to Annie. "How do you live with this?"

Annie sighed deeply and looked seriously at her sister and aunt. "It's hard," she said. "But they can't help themselves."

"Oh, man," Meg said. "I don't feel *that* bad about it. Just show them to us already."

Juliet laughed as she knelt beside the bags and unzipped first one and then the other. Out of one of them she pulled a blue dress with a white apron.

"Here's Alice," she said, handing the costume to Annie to hold up.

Aunt Sarah looked approvingly at the dress. "Very nice," she said. "With some black shoes and white socks, that will be perfect."

"And here's the groom," Juliet announced. She had taken out a purple velvet jacket and a plain white shirt. "But that's not the best part." Again she reached into the bag, and this time she emerged with a large hat that resembled a top hat that had been sat upon and badly smashed.

"That's perfect!" Annie said. "It looks just like the one the Mad Hatter wore."

"It still needs some work," Juliet said. "But this is basically it."

"Where's mine?" Meg asked impatiently, looking meaningfully at the second bag.

"Coming right up," said Juliet. She rummaged around in the bag and pulled out a vest made of red plaid material and a jacket made out of green plaid material.

"I brought some fuzzy material for making ears, too," she told Meg. "And wait until you see the nose and whiskers my friend Todd came up with. The man is a *genius* with latex."

Another trip into the bag revealed bolts of fuzzy purple and pink material that Juliet announced she was going to fashion Becka's Cheshire Cat costume out of during the week. She also showed them the gorgeous red, black, and white velvet dress she'd fashioned for the Queen of Hearts.

"And now for the best part," she said, looking at Annie.

Annie held her breath. She'd been wondering what her Caterpillar costume might look like. Juliet had refused to give her any hints.

Juliet pulled what looked like a length of greenish blue silk from the bag. She shook it and Annie,

Meg, and Aunt Sarah all gasped in surprise. The silk was actually a kind of body suit. Attached to either side were six short arms, also made out of silk, that had been stuffed so that they stood out from the main body of the costume.

"What do you think?" Juliet asked.

"I think it's amazing," said Annie, taking the costume and holding it up to herself. The twelve arms jiggled around, making her laugh. "I can't wait to try it on."

"You and I will have to work on some kind of mask or head thing," Juliet told her sister. "Otherwise you'll just look like Annie the Amazing Worm Girl or something." She looked at Meg and Aunt Sarah, who were also admiring their costumes. "Actually, none of these are totally done," she said. "I'll be working on all the details this week. So if there's anything you don't like, just say so."

"They're wonderful," Aunt Sarah said, putting down her dress and giving Juliet a big hug. "I can't thank you enough for all of this."

"It was my pleasure," Juliet told her. "Believe me, working on these was a lot more interesting than making sixteen identical bowling shirts for the theater people."

"They're doing a show about bowling?" asked Meg. "That sounds boring."

Juliet laughed. "It's even more boring than that," she told her sister. "They actually *are* bowling. It's for their league. They wanted something unique to wear.

We drew straws for who had to make them, and I lost. After making all of those, coming up with White Rabbit and Caterpillar costumes was a picnic."

"Speaking of food," said Aunt Sarah. "Are you all ready for dinner?"

"We're having fajitas," Annie told Juliet. "I thought that would be fun."

"Sounds great," Juliet said. "Let me just put these costumes up in my room and I'll be down."

"I'll help," Meg said.

The two of them gathered up the various articles of clothing, put them back into the bags, and carried everything upstairs. While they were doing that, Annie and her aunt went to the kitchen and began getting everything ready.

"She's so nice," Aunt Sarah said to Annie. "I hope I'm not staring at her too much. It's just so strange seeing someone who weighed eight pounds the last time I saw her. I don't think it's quite sunk in yet that she's really Peter and Chloe's daughter."

"I know what you mean," Annie said as she began cutting up strips of yellow and red peppers for the fajitas. "Every so often I stop and think 'That's my big sister over there.'"

"Things have changed so much since last year," Aunt Sarah said as she took some beef from the refrigerator. "For all of us."

Annie hesitated a moment. "Are you scared at all?" she asked her aunt.

"Scared?" Aunt Sarah asked, putting the meat on

a cutting board and beginning to slice it into thin strips. "Of what?"

Annie shrugged. "I was just thinking about something that Kate said the other day," she said. "She said that if she were you, she'd be a little worried about giving up her independence. You know, with Grayson moving in and all."

Aunt Sarah laughed, surprising Annie. When her aunt saw the look on Annie's face she put down her knife. "I'm sorry," she said. "I wasn't laughing at you. I was just thinking about how that sounds exactly like something I would have said myself when I was your age."

"But you don't feel that way now?" Annie asked her.

"No," her aunt replied. "And I'll tell you why. Independence doesn't have to mean doing things on your own. You can have a boyfriend or husband or partner and still be very independent. You can have a family and be independent. Your mother was one of the most independent women I've ever known, but she was also a totally devoted mother to you and Meg. She made time for herself. She did the things that were important to her. I don't plan on putting part of myself in storage just because I'm marrying Grayson. I feel as if I'm adding even more to my life by having him—and Becka—in it. It's the same way I felt when you and Meg came to live here."

Annie thought about that. She had never really

considered how her aunt's life must have changed after she and her sister moved in. She'd been very young then, and only worried about herself. Now, though, she found herself wondering how her aunt's life might have been different had she and Meg never come to live with her. Would she have gotten married earlier? Would she have children of her own? Suddenly, Annie felt a little guilty.

"I know what you're thinking," Aunt Sarah said. "And you can just stop. I wouldn't trade having you and Meg grow up here with me for anything. I miss Peter and Chloe every single day of my life. But I'm also thankful every day of my life that we're a family. A family that seems to just keep growing," she added thoughtfully as Meg and Juliet came into the kitchen.

"Can we help?" Juliet asked.

"Actually, everything is just about ready to go," Annie said, giving her aunt a quick hug as she dried her hands on a towel and went to get the tortillas. "Just sit down and I'll start cooking."

Annie fired up the stove and cooked the meat and vegetables, spooning them onto waiting plates as soon as they were ready. When everyone had their fajitas, they sat down and started eating. Soon they were eating and talking, lost in the pleasures of food and conversation.

When they were done, everyone helped clean up. Then Aunt Sarah went to do some work on a project she was working on for a client, while Meg went to her room to read. Annie and Juliet stayed to finish washing the last few dishes.

"Can I ask you something?" said Juliet as Annie handed her a dish to dry.

"Sure," Annie answered.

"I've been wanting to ask you about your Wicca class," Juliet said. "But I didn't want you to think I was being nosy or anything."

"No," said Annie. "It's okay. What do you want to know?"

Juliet put the dish away in the cabinet with the others. "I was just wondering—can anyone do it, or do you have to, like, have witch blood or something?"

Annie laughed. "Witch blood?" she said. "Where did you come up with that?"

Juliet looked a little embarrassed. "I have this friend," she said. "I mentioned to her that my sister was into Wicca, and she said that we must have witch blood in our family and that if you do then I do, too."

Annie turned off the water and dried her hands. "There *are* families where being a witch is something that is handed down from parents to children," Annie said. "But no, that's not how it usually works. It's not like inheriting blue eyes or anything like that."

"So our mother wasn't a witch?" Juliet asked.

Annie sighed. "I can't answer that," she said. "I don't have any reason to think that she was, but you never know. I do know that she painted that picture in my room because she saw a woman standing by my crib when I was a baby."

"So you think that *you* were destined to be a witch?" said Juliet.

Annie thought about the question for a moment. She was, when it came down to it, a scientist. She liked things that could be explained through experimentation and facts and results. Witchcraft, at least at first glance, was none of those things. It was about intentions, and working with powers that couldn't be seen, and believing in things that couldn't be proven. Yet being a part of Wicca had changed her life more dramatically, and more positively, than anything else she could think of. It had helped her make friendships. It had helped her deal with the deaths of her parents. It had reunited her with her sister. It had shown her parts of herself she never knew existed—strengths she had and abilities she could use to change her life for the better.

"Yes," she said. "I think I was destined to be a witch."

CHAPTER 12

If I win, it means I'm making the right decision. Kate sat in front of her computer on Sunday afternoon, playing Solitaire. She'd decided that if she won the game she was currently playing, it would be a sign that she'd made the right choice in selecting the Coven of the Green Wood. She very seldom won, so she'd convinced herself that successfully completing a round would be a dramatic portent of good things to come. As she moved the cards around, forming rows and trying to get all of the cards of similar suits stacked onto the four piles at the top of the screen, she tried not to remind herself that Solitaire was largely a game of luck, and that whether she won or not had very little to do with anything other than how the cards had been stacked.

She was currently stuck. There was a red seven sitting on top of the largest pile, and she knew that the ace of spades she needed desperately to find was underneath it. She needed a black eight to show up so she could move the seven and get things going again.

She clicked on the draw pile, turning over three new cards, and saw the eight she needed pop up.

Perfect, she thought happily, adding the eight to the waiting nine of diamonds and placing the seven of hearts on top of that. *And there's the ace of spades*, she cheered. She moved the ace to the remaining open spot and began putting the cards in order. A few plays later, she had completed the hand. She watched as the images of the cards bounced around her computer screen in a celebratory display, then she shut off the program.

She'd won the game, but somehow it wasn't the thrill she'd expected it to be. *Come on*, she ordered herself, *now you know you made the right choice*. But had she? She had to wonder. Yes, she'd won at Solitaire. But what did that prove? It was just a game. *It could just be a stupid coincidence*, she admonished herself. *You might as well have said that if the phone rings right now it's a sign.*

The phone rang. Kate looked at it, rolled her eyes, and picked it up.

"Hello?"

"Hey." Kate heard Tyler on the other end. He sounded particularly happy.

"What's up?" asked Kate, unsure of how to react. It was the first time she'd spoken with Tyler since agreeing to join his coven.

"Nothing," Tyler said. "I was just wondering what you were doing."

"Oh," Kate replied. "Well, um, nothing really." She looked at the computer screen, relieved that

Tyler had no way of knowing that she'd been using a stupid card game to justify her decision to join the coven.

"In that case, want to get together?"

Kate was caught off guard. Why did Tyler want to get together with her? Was it just simply because—in their own strange way—they'd sort of made up the other night and were friends again? Or did he think there was something more going on?

"Just to hang out and talk," he said, as if reading her mind. "It's not a date or anything."

"You got that right," said Kate, feeling that she needed to reinforce the idea that she and Tyler were most definitely not getting back on the dating track.

"I was thinking we could meet at the wharf and maybe get coffee or something," Tyler said, either not caring that she'd snapped at him or choosing to ignore it. "You know, talk about the coven and stuff like that."

Kate hesitated. She wasn't sure that spending a lot of time with Tyler was a good idea at the moment, especially after the long period of separation they'd had. But she *did* have a few things she wanted to ask him about the coven. *And it's just coffee*, she told herself reassuringly.

"Okay," she said. "I'll meet you at The Last Drop."

"Great," Tyler responded. "See you."

Kate hung up. As she changed clothes and

prepared to go meet her ex-boyfriend, she thought about all the excuses she could have come up with for not going. *It's almost like you want to see him, just to see what will happen*, she told herself sternly.

"That's ridiculous," she said aloud. Things between her and Tyler were over. She was sure of that.

Then why are you taking your new red shirt out of the closet? Kate looked and saw that she had indeed removed the shirt she'd bought while shopping with her Aunt Netty the week before. Had she really been thinking about wearing it for Tyler? The very idea made her angry, and she put the shirt back immediately, instead deciding to wear a blue one she knew he wasn't particularly crazy about.

She hastily applied some lipstick and mascara, resenting the fact that she was putting even that much makeup on. Suddenly she felt that any effort she made to make herself look good was something she was doing for Tyler's benefit, and she didn't want to do that. *This is just coffee*, she repeated to herself as she grabbed her coat and left the house. *Get over it*.

Throughout the entire bus ride into town she had to remind herself that meeting Tyler was no big deal, nothing to get excited about. At each new stop she would watch the doors opening and think, *You could get out here. You could catch a bus home and just forget about it.* But she could never get herself to stand up and walk down the aisle to the door. All she could do was sit and watch the city going by outside her window.

Finally they reached the wharf and she got off the bus. She saw Tyler standing on the pier, leaning against the railing and looking off into the distance. She walked toward him, not rushing, and when she reached him she leaned up against the railing beside him.

"What are you looking at?" she asked.

Tyler turned and smiled at her. "Just the ocean," he said. "It looks like a storm is coming." He looked at her for a moment. "Nice shirt," he added.

Kate ignored the compliment and looked out to sea. Indeed, the sky was growing darker out where the sky met the water. The waves lapping up against the pilings of the pier were stronger than usual, and farther out she could see whitecaps. Something was indeed coming. *We'll probably have rain tonight*, Kate thought vaguely.

"Ready for some coffee?" asked Tyler.

Kate shrugged and fell into step beside him as he walked in the direction of The Last Drop. Neither of them said anything as Tyler opened the door and they stepped inside the tiny coffee shop. Kate located a free table and made for it, Tyler in tow. She placed her coat on the back of one of the chairs and sat down. Tyler sat across from her.

"Well, this feels familiar," Tyler said, referring to the fact that he and Kate had sometimes come to this very coffee shop when they were dating, usually to discuss a movie they'd just seen or to look at something they'd just bought.

"I was here the other day with Sasha," Kate remarked, wanting Tyler to know that he shouldn't think of The Last Drop as "their" place or anything.

"What can I get you?" The waiter appeared, making further immediate conversation unnecessary.

"How about a piece of lemon cheesecake and a cup of peppermint tea," Tyler said. "Kate?"

"I'll have a cup of coffee, black, and a chocolate chip muffin," Kate told the waiter, who wrote everything down, took their menus, and departed.

"Black coffee," Tyler remarked. "That's a change."

Kate nodded. "What can I say?" she replied. "I'm unpredictable."

"I won't argue with that," Tyler said. "So, are you excited about initiation now that you know which coven you'll be going for?"

"I don't really know what to think about it," said Kate. "I honestly haven't thought about it much beyond the part about having to choose a coven. What's going to happen?"

Tyler gave her a mysterious smile. "No way," he said. "I'm not telling you a thing. Half the fun of initiation is not knowing what's going to happen."

Kate wanted to press him some more, but she let it go. To her surprise, she was remarkably uninterested in what was in store for her at initiation. *You should be more excited about this*, she told herself. But for some reason she wasn't.

"I have some questions for you," she said abruptly, not wanting to think about why her enthusiasm for the approaching ceremony seemed to have faded.

"Do I need a lawyer?" Tyler asked, holding up his hands in a gesture of surrender.

"About the coven," Kate said shortly. "For one thing, do you have full moon rituals every month?"

"More or less," Tyler said. "We like to try to have them as close to the actual full moon as possible, and sometimes that just doesn't work out for one reason or another and we skip a month."

Kate nodded. "Do you guys do magic at every circle?" she asked.

"No," Tyler said. "In fact, we don't do a lot of magic in our circles unless there's a specific thing we're trying to accomplish. Individual members usually do magical work on their own, and the circles are more for ritual and celebrating the sabbats."

"Okay," said Kate, as if she were an interviewer and his answer had satisfied her. "Are you trying to get me to go out with you again?"

Tyler's head snapped back and he looked at Kate in surprise. She looked back, her gaze steady as she refused to back down.

"Um," Tyler said, clearly caught off guard.

"You'd better tell me the truth," Kate said. "And you have five seconds, otherwise I'm leaving again. Five. Four. Three. Two."

"Okay," Tyler said before she could reach one.

"Why did you ask me that?"

"That's not an answer," said Kate. "Time's up."

She stood, but Tyler jumped up and caught her by the wrist. "Just sit down," he said.

Kate hesitated a moment, then took her seat. She sat in silence as Tyler sat down and brought his chair closer to the table. He looked uncomfortable, and he kept playing with his napkin, worrying it between his fingers.

"Maybe I am sort of hoping that you'll give us another chance," he said finally.

Kate let out a long sigh. "I should have known," she said.

"Wait a minute," said Tyler. "Why am I a bad guy all of a sudden just because I'd like to see us give it a try?"

"Because you shouldn't have used the coven to try to get me back," Kate said.

Inconveniently, the waiter appeared right at that moment with their orders. Both Tyler and Kate avoided looking at him as he set their cups and plates down. Sensing some tension at the table, the waiter made a quick retreat, after which Kate took a sip of her coffee, not bothering to blow on it to cool it and not caring that it burned her tongue a little.

"You shouldn't have said you wanted me in the coven when what you really wanted was to get me to go out with you," she said.

"That's not why I asked you to join the coven," Tyler protested.

"You just said—" Kate began.

"No," Tyler said, interrupting her. "What I said was that yes, I would like to go out with you again. I didn't say that I used the invitation to join the coven as a way to get you to do that. If you don't want to go out with me again, that's fine. You've already made it clear on more than one occasion that you don't want to. But I still think you'd be a good addition to the coven, and even though it would be hard for me to have you there knowing that you don't want to be with me, I'd do it because that's more important than having a date."

It was Kate's turn to be taken aback. "Oh," she finally managed to say.

"Did you *really* think that I would use my coven to try to lure you into some kind of trap?" Tyler asked.

Kate nodded. "The thought crossed my mind," she said.

Tyler leaned back in his chair. "Kate, apart from my family, the coven is the most important thing in my life. I would never use my involvement in it—or in Wicca—to try to get someone to do something she didn't want to do. You of all people should know how dangerous that is."

Kate knew that Tyler was referring to the fact that she had once used a spell to get a guy to fall for her. That incident had caused her a lot of trouble and pain, but it had also been the reason for her getting involved both with the Wicca study group and with Tyler. Still, Tyler was right. She should have known that he would never do anything to try to manipulate her.

"I guess I kind of owe you an apology," said Kate sheepishly.

Tyler took a bite of his cheesecake. "Apology accepted," he said.

"It's just that I was having doubts about joining the coven," Kate explained. "Something was holding me back. I thought about it and thought about it, and—"

Again, Tyler interrupted her. "And you couldn't possibly accept that I suggested you join because you're good at ritual and magic," he said.

"Well, yeah," said Kate. "I guess."

"Some things about you haven't changed at all, Kate," Tyler said. "You're still doubting yourself."

Kate ignored him, taking a bite of her muffin. The chocolate chips were warm and soft, and the taste spread through her mouth, mingling with the coffee. "I know I'll be a good witch," she said matter-of-factly.

"I know you will be, too," Tyler said. "So stop thinking that everything I do is to try to get back together, okay?"

Kate nodded. "I'll try," she said.

"Good," Tyler said. "Now, let me ask *you* a question. Do you want to go to a movie this weekend?"

"I guess—" Kate began, then stopped. She shut her eyes. *I can't believe I said that*, she thought, wanting to die of embarrassment. When she opened her eyes, Tyler was looking at her, a self-satisfied smirk on his face.

"That was a trick question," Kate said, trying to keep her voice calm. "And anyway, I can't go to a movie this weekend. Annie's aunt is getting married, and we're all helping out."

"Fine," Tyler said. "There's always the weekend after. The point is, *you* want to go."

"Just because I said I would go to a movie with you does *not* mean I have any intention of getting back together with you, Tyler Decklin," Kate said.

"You used my whole name," Tyler said, taking another bite of cheesecake. He pointed his fork at Kate. "You like me."

"Like a rash," said Kate, chomping on a bite of her muffin. What was going on? Had she really just admitted to Tyler that she might actually consider going out with him again? *That's nuts*, she told herself. *You've told him over and over that it's over.* She laughed silently at her repeated use of the word *over*. *But it is over*, she insisted.

"If you didn't at least have *some* interest in maybe, possibly, perhaps getting back together with me, you wouldn't have answered so quickly," Tyler teased her. "That was your subconscious talking. You said the first thing you thought of—which is also usually the thing you secretly want to do," he added.

"Excuse me," Kate said. "Which one of us used that trick first? If I recall, it was *me*."

"I only steal from the best," replied Tyler.

There was a long pause during which the two of them ate their desserts and sipped their drinks. Then Tyler pushed his plate away. "Seriously," he said. "Would you at least think about going out on a date with me?"

Kate slowly chewed the last bite of her muffin. She knew that when she was done with it she would have no excuse not to answer Tyler, so as she ground the chocolate chips into the finest paste possible she held a debate with herself.

You told him it was totally over, she thought.

It is over.

Then why are you even playing around with him on this? You're letting him think that maybe there's a possibility that the two of you might get together again.

It's just a movie.

Just a movie becomes just dinner, and then just a concert, and then he's just your boyfriend again.

But he's being so nice. Maybe I was too hard on him.

You're just feeling that way because he asked you to be in the coven.

So? Maybe that's what it took for me to realize I made a mistake.

No, now you're making the mistake. You were right when you dumped him.

Kate listened to the two halves of her brain fighting it out. She wasn't sure which one she was rooting for. The intellectual part of her knew that refusing to get back together with Tyler was the right thing. But the part of her that still remembered how much she'd loved looking into his golden eyes and seeing them looking back was starting to give in.

"One movie," she said. "We each pay for ourselves. And *no* hand holding or attempted hand holding."

"I can accept those terms," Tyler said after careful consideration.

"I'm sure this is the stupidest thing I've ever agreed to," Kate said as she took out her wallet and counted some bills to pay for her coffee and muffin.

Tyler paid his half and the two of them got up to go. As they left The Last Drop, Kate was surprised to see Annie and Cooper walking toward them. Her first instinct was to duck back inside. For some reason, she didn't want her friends to see her with Tyler. But Annie spied them and waved.

"Hey," she said as she and Cooper reached the shop. "I called you a while ago to see if you wanted to come out with us, but you weren't home. Now I know why." She glanced at Tyler. "Hi, Tyler," she said a little hesitantly.

Tyler nodded at Annie and waved a hand at Cooper.

"What has you two out tonight?" Cooper asked.

Kate looked at Tyler. "We just got together to talk about some stuff," Kate said, knowing it was a lame explanation.

"About class," Tyler added quickly.

"Class?" Annie said, sounding as if she didn't believe it.

"Yeah," Tyler said, sounding, Kate thought, way too cheerful. "About initiation. Covens."

Kate cringed. She didn't want to hurt Cooper's feelings by talking about initiation. But Tyler, who didn't know how awful Cooper felt about being excluded from the upcoming ritual, had said exactly the wrong thing without meaning to.

Sensing the silence, Tyler tried to fill it. "Yeah," he said. "I think I've convinced Kate to join the Coven of the Green Wood."

Annie looked at Kate. Her face wore an expression of confusion and hurt combined. "You didn't tell me you'd decided," she said.

Kate looked at Annie's wounded expression, then at Cooper, who was suddenly preoccupied with looking at her fingernails. She also shot Tyler a glance, but she knew that he couldn't help her. She was on her own.

"I just kind of decided tonight," she said.

"Oh," Annie replied, looking from Tyler to Kate and back again. "Okay."

"You know what," said Tyler, looking at his watch. "I told my mom I would be back fifteen minutes ago. I should leave."

"Bye," Kate said stiffly. She didn't want her friends to think that her meeting with Tyler had been anything else but class-related.

Tyler said good-night to Annie and Cooper and walked quickly away. Kate stood there, looking at her friends.

"Actually, it's interesting that we ran into you," Annie said. "Cooper wants to talk to us about initiation."

"Really?" Kate said, genuinely surprised.

Cooper shrugged. "I just had an idea is all," she said. "But if you've already made up your mind, it doesn't matter."

"No," Kate said. "I'd like to hear what you're thinking."

Cooper nodded toward The Last Drop. "We were going to go in here," she said.

Kate nodded. "That's fine," she said. "I didn't really have anything. Just coffee."

They turned and walked into the shop. Seeing Kate again, the waiter gave her a puzzled look but didn't say anything. As he walked the three of them to the same table she and Tyler had just vacated, Kate wondered what her friends wanted to talk to her about. *Maybe agreeing to go out with Tyler* wasn't *the stupidest thing you've done tonight*, she thought uneasily.

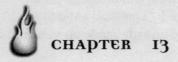

CHAPTER 13

The three friends sat around the table, not saying anything as they looked at the menus. Finally, Cooper put hers down. "I don't know what either of you have decided about initiation and which covens you're thinking of joining," she said, looking particularly hard at Kate. "But I have something to say about it."

Annie and Kate exchanged glances. They put their menus down and waited for Cooper to continue.

"I still don't understand exactly why I wasn't offered initiation," Cooper said. "But it doesn't really matter. The point is, I wasn't. So as I see it, I have three choices. One—I can stop practicing Wicca altogether. Two—I can look for another coven that will have me." She paused.

"What's number three?" Annie asked her.

Cooper took a breath. "Three—I can start my own coven."

Kate and Annie regarded her with surprise. "Start

your own coven?" Kate said. "Can you do that?"

Cooper nodded. "There's no reason you can't," she said. "People who live in areas where there are no other Wiccan groups do it all the time. It's not like you have to buy a franchise or something."

"You're really thinking of starting your own coven?" said Annie.

"Yeah, I am," Cooper answered. "I think I'm ready to be a witch. I *know* I'm ready. Just because Sophia and the other teachers seem to disagree with me is no reason not to do it. It's just their opinion. They aren't the Supreme Court of witchdom or anything; they're just people."

"But they have a lot of experience," Kate said.

Cooper gave her a hard look. "Meaning they must be right about me, is that it?" she asked.

Kate shook her head. "I didn't say that," she said carefully. "I'm just saying that maybe they know a little more than we do. If you start your own coven, you'd be on your own."

"It's not like I don't know how to do a circle, or work magic," countered Cooper. "I've been doing it all just fine for a year now."

"But you need more than one person to have a coven," Annie said. "Where would you find other witches?"

Cooper looked at Annie and then at Kate. At first her friends just stared back, not understanding. Then Annie realized what Cooper was implying.

"You want *us* to be in this coven," she said. "Is that it?"

"Why not?" said Cooper, leaning forward and talking excitedly. "We've already been working together for a year. We're practically a coven anyway. This would just be making it official."

"But none of us are initiated witches," said Kate.

"Why is that such a big deal?" Cooper retorted. "Don't you think we've accomplished some great stuff already? Do you think having someone initiate you is going to make you a better witch?"

Kate looked down. "No," she said. "It wouldn't make me a *better* witch. It's just that—" She hesitated, looking like she didn't know what to say.

"Just what?" Cooper demanded.

"I think what Kate is trying to say is that while we know initiation won't make us any better, it *is* what we've all been working toward this past year," said Annie.

"Is it?" asked Cooper. "Is it really just all about initiation?"

Annie and Kate looked at her curiously.

"See, that's how I was looking at it, too," Cooper said. Now that she had their attention, she was ready to hit them with what she thought was her most powerful argument. "All year I've been focused on initiation. It was like this big goal for me. But then when it was taken away from me, I started to think about things differently. This year hasn't been about initiation; it's been about learning. And being initiated into a coven doesn't really mean we've learned anything. Sophia. Archer. None of them can see inside of us to know how we've changed. They don't know everything we've been through. Only we do. The three of us went through all of this together, and I think we should stay together."

Cooper opened the backpack she'd carried with her and took out the book she'd been reading. "Jane gave this to me," she said, putting the book on the table. "She thought maybe I would be interested in reading about being a solitary. But the more I read the book, the more I thought about how maybe we could form our own coven. If one person can self-initiate, there's no reason a group of people can't."

Kate and Annie looked at the book. Kate picked it up and leafed through it. "It just never occurred to me that we might be able to create our own coven," she said.

"It hadn't occurred to me, either," Cooper told her. "But the book gave me the idea. And then I started to think about my grandmother, and about how she practiced magic without ever having a coven."

"Are you sure she didn't?" Kate asked, handing the book to Annie.

"I talked to my mother about it," Cooper said.

Again her friends looked surprised. "I thought she wouldn't discuss that," said Annie.

"She wasn't crazy about it," Cooper said. "But I

got a little more out of her. She said that as far as she knows, my grandmother never did anything with a group."

"So she was a solitary," Kate said. "There are lots of solitaries."

"The point is, my grandmother didn't need someone to put a stamp of approval on her magic, and neither do we," Cooper said. "We could start our own coven and keep on working together the way we have been. Nothing would be any different."

At that moment the waiter arrived to take their orders. There was a pause in the conversation as each of them ordered. Then, when the waiter left, Cooper looked at her friends. "So, what do you think?"

Annie was the first to respond. "I agree with you that you don't need someone to tell you what you are when it comes to spirituality," she said. "I think that if you choose to accept a set of beliefs, and if you're dedicated to following those beliefs, then you're whatever you say you are. I don't think going through an initiation ceremony will *make* me a real witch. I think I already am one because I follow Wiccan principles and I want to spend my life walking the Wiccan path." She paused. "But I do think the ritual is important to me personally. To me it symbolizes completing the first part of my journey."

"And what about joining a coven?" Cooper asked her.

Annie shrugged. "That part I'm less sure about," she said. "To tell the truth, none of the covens we've heard about have seemed absolutely perfect for me. Not that there's anything wrong with them or anything. It's just that none of them have stood out as being completely right for me."

"So you'd be open to forming our own coven?" Cooper pressed.

"I'd have to think about that," Annie said.

Cooper moved on to Kate. "What about you?" she asked. "Was Tyler telling the truth? Have you already decided to join their coven?"

"You make it sound like a crime," Kate remarked.

"No," Cooper said. "I'm just asking. He made it sound like a done deal."

"Well, I do think the Coven of the Green Wood is a great coven," Kate said.

"And what about Tyler being in it?" Annie asked her.

"I don't think that's a problem," said Kate.

"Are you two getting back together?" Cooper asked.

Kate didn't answer right away, and her hesitation caused Cooper and Annie to look at each other in suspicion.

"Something's up," Annie remarked to Cooper.

"I just said I'd go to a movie with him," objected Kate. "Stop trying to make me feel guilty."

"No one is trying to make you feel guilty,"

Cooper told her. "We're just asking."

"I like the Coven of the Green Wood because of its emphasis on teaching," Kate said defensively. "Annie, I told you that last week."

"She did," Annie confirmed, looking at Cooper and nodding.

"Okay," Cooper said. "So I guess you've made up your mind."

"You make it sound like I'm a bad person for wanting to be part of an established coven," Kate said. "I didn't say I wouldn't want to be in a coven with the two of you."

Cooper grinned. "So you *would* be interested in starting our own?"

"I didn't say that either," Kate replied. "I said I would like to be in a coven with both of you—if there was a coven we could all join."

"But they're not letting me into a coven!" Cooper said. "That's the whole point. We can't be in the same coven if I'm not even allowed to join one. That's why I think we should start our own. That way we can all be together."

Kate didn't say anything in response, so Cooper looked at Annie. "*You* think starting our own coven is a good idea, right?" she said. "I mean, you said it didn't matter if other people told us we were witches or not."

"That's true," replied Annie. "I don't think it matters. But I also said that initiation was important to *me*."

"Meaning you're siding with Kate," Cooper said. "I get it."

"I'm not siding with anyone," Annie told her. "I'm saying that I think it's important for me personally to go through with the initiation process."

"Which still leaves me out in the cold," Cooper said, sounding angry. "Look, I'm sorry I brought this up. I don't know what I was thinking."

The waiter arrived with their drinks, giving them all time to think before resuming the conversation.

"I understand that you're frustrated," said Annie. "I would be, too. And I really do think that there's no reason you or anybody else can't call herself a witch if she feels she is one. But I also don't want to give up this initiation experience. Maybe that's selfish of me, but it's how I feel."

Cooper nodded. She really *did* understand what Annie was saying. At the same time, part of her desperately wanted her friends to declare their loyalty to her by agreeing to start their own coven.

"I feel like anything I say is going to be wrong," Kate said after a moment. "Cooper, I would love to be in a coven with you. But I can't say that I don't also really want to be in the Coven of the Green Wood."

Cooper took a swig of the cappuccino she'd ordered. She was angry at herself. She'd allowed herself to imagine that her friends would readily agree with her proposal and that everything would suddenly take care of itself. Instead, she had shown them just how upset she was about not being part of a coven, and still she wasn't getting what she wanted.

"We can still work together," Annie said to Cooper.

"Just don't," Cooper replied. She looked at her friend. "I know you're trying to make me feel better, but it's just making me feel worse," she said. "I already feel like the kid nobody chooses for their softball team."

Cooper drank the rest of her cappuccino in three quick gulps. She knew she would regret it when the caffeine hit her system, but she needed to get out of the coffee shop.

"I really have to go," she said, putting money down. "I'm sorry I made you guys feel bad about this."

She grabbed her coat from the back of her chair and left before her friends could stop her. Outside, she walked quickly, anxious to get to her car.

What was I thinking? she asked herself as she walked. She felt like a fool. *And it's all Sophia's fault*, a voice in her head reminded her. If it hadn't been for Sophia and the others, she would be looking forward to initiation with Kate and Annie instead of going home alone to lick her wounds.

Suddenly she stopped walking and turned around. She began to go in the other direction, walking quickly and purposefully. She turned the corner at the wharf and headed directly for Crones' Circle. Before she could think about what she was doing, she pushed open the door and went inside. She hadn't stepped foot in the store since running out the night of her rejection. It felt strange being there again.

Sophia was standing behind the counter, helping a customer. When she saw Cooper standing in the store she smiled at her. Cooper didn't return the gesture. She stood, pretending to look at a stack of new books, until the man Sophia was waiting on left.

"It's good to see you here again," Sophia said, coming up to Cooper.

"I just want to know why," Cooper said, facing her. "I want to know *exactly* why I wasn't offered initiation."

"I thought we'd been over this," answered Sophia. "We just don't think you're quite ready."

Cooper nodded. "But you don't have any real reason," she said angrily.

Sophia bit her lip, regarding Cooper for a moment. "There are some things you can't measure," she said finally. "I can't say that there's any one thing you did or didn't do that influenced our decision. It's just a feeling we had."

"Oh, a feeling," Cooper said. "Well, I have feelings, too, and what I'm feeling right now is that the whole bunch of you are full of it. I worked my butt off in this class. I *know* I'm ready to be a witch. And

I don't need you or anyone else to say that I'm ready."

"Is that what you came here to say?" asked Sophia quietly.

Cooper nodded. "And just so you know," she added, "I don't need to be initiated to know what I am. You can keep me out of your covens, but you can't stop me from being a witch. And even if Kate and Annie don't want to start a coven with me, that doesn't mean I can't find people who will."

"You were thinking of starting a coven with Annie and Kate?" said Sophia.

"Yes," Cooper told her. She hadn't meant to drag her friends into the conversation. She'd only wanted to give Sophia a piece of her mind. But now that she'd said it, she had to continue. "I asked them to forget about initiation and start a coven with me," she said. "But it's important to them to go through with your stupid ritual, so that's what they're doing."

Sophia nodded. "I see," she said. "Do you really think our initiation ritual is stupid?"

Cooper looked at her former teacher. Sophia had done a lot of nice things for her. She'd helped her on more than one occasion, and until being turned down for initiation Cooper had respected her as one of the smartest, kindest people she knew. But now she had said something cruel to Sophia, and she felt bad about that.

"No," she said, trying to sound less hostile. "I

don't think it's stupid. But I don't think it makes anyone a witch, either," she added stubbornly.

Cooper was surprised to see Sophia smile. The smile grew until Sophia was laughing. Cooper didn't understand what was so funny, and she felt as if she were being made fun of, which irritated her.

"I have to say," Sophia said when she'd stopped chuckling, "your timing is perfect."

"What do you mean?" Cooper asked, confused.

"It's just like you to wait until almost the last minute," Sophia told her.

Cooper still didn't understand. "Wait for what?" she said.

Sophia took a deep breath and nodded toward the back of the store. "Come with me," she said. "We need to talk."

Sophia turned and walked into the back room. Not wanting to, but curious about what was going on, Cooper followed. Sophia sat in one of the armchairs and motioned for Cooper to sit in the other. Cooper did, but sat stiffly, still wary about the situation.

"It's true that we didn't think you were ready for initiation," Sophia told her in a gentle voice. "You didn't exactly meet your challenge."

"What do you mean?" Cooper said, getting angry again. "I stood in front of all of those people during the play and forgot my lines! But I got through it. I faced my greatest fear."

Sophia shook her head. "That wasn't your greatest fear," she said. "It was a big one, but it wasn't your greatest one."

Cooper shook her head. "If that wasn't it, then what is?" she asked, totally confused.

"Not being initiated," said Sophia simply.

Cooper stared at her. Slowly, she began to understand what Sophia was telling her. "You mean you told me I wasn't going to be initiated because you knew that was what I would be most afraid of," she said.

"Yes," Sophia said. "Cooper, all year you were one of the strongest students in the class, perhaps the strongest. But your one stumbling block has always been your tendency to be a loner. You've made great strides in working with others. We've all seen that. To tell the truth, at first even we weren't sure that the incident with forgetting lines *wasn't* your challenge. But the more we thought about it, the more we knew that a student with your abilities would never be given such an easy assignment. Something just wasn't right about it."

"So you decided to make up another test for me," Cooper said.

"We decided that for you a real test would be being told you couldn't have something you'd worked so hard to achieve, something you wanted even though in many ways it was totally against everything you've always stood for. For you to want to be part of a group, and to want the acceptance that an initiation ritual implies, you would have to overcome all of the things you've built up to keep yourself safe from being hurt. And *that* would be the greatest fear, and the greatest challenge, you could face."

Cooper was stunned. She couldn't believe what Sophia was saying.

"I was set up?" she said.

Again, Sophia laughed. "In a way," she said.

"That is so *not* fair," exclaimed Cooper angrily.

"No one ever said magic was fair," said Sophia.

Cooper shook her head. "So what are you saying?" she asked. "What's the deal?"

"You passed," Sophia told her.

"Passed?" repeated Cooper.

"Yes," said Sophia. "You came here to tell me that you were willing to go ahead with your journey even though we'd told you you couldn't. You recognized that the initiation ritual is largely symbolic. You saw the witch within yourself and you let her out with no help from us."

"I did, didn't I?" Cooper said. Somehow when Sophia said it, it all made sense.

"You faced your greatest fear and you didn't let it stop you from doing what you knew in your heart you needed to do," Sophia told her.

Suddenly, Cooper realized what it all meant. "Does this mean I'm back in?" she asked excitedly.

Sophia nodded. "If you're interested, we'd love for you to be part of the initiation ritual."

Cooper's heart was pounding in her chest, she was so excited. She'd passed! She was being offered initiation after all. She wasn't a failure.

Wait a minute, a voice in her head said. *Five minutes ago you were saying that initiation wasn't important.*

She thought about that. No, it wasn't important to her to have someone else's approval. She was pleased that she'd met the challenge of facing her greatest fear, even if she hadn't realized that's what she was doing, but it didn't change how she felt about things. She still didn't think being initiated along with the others would make her any more of a real witch than she already was.

Still, it might be fun, she thought. She had to admit, there was a part of her that would really like to stand with Kate and Annie and finish what they'd started together a year and a day before. She didn't, however, want to give Sophia the satisfaction of saying yes too easily.

"I'll think about it," she said, trying to sound cool.

Sophia smiled. "You do that," she said. "But think fast. Tomorrow is the last class."

Cooper nodded. "I'll be there," she said as she stood up and prepared to leave.

"Oh, and Cooper," Sophia said.

Cooper turned around.

"Good work," Sophia said admiringly.

CHAPTER 14

"Welcome to your last class before initiation," Sophia said the following evening. She looked around the room. "The next time the seven—I mean eight," she corrected herself, looking at Cooper, who was seated between Annie and Kate on the floor, "of you are all together it will be as fully initiated witches."

The class members gave little cheers and smiled at one another. Annie looked at Cooper. She still couldn't quite believe what Cooper had told her and Kate that morning at school. At first she'd thought that perhaps Cooper was joking, but when she'd realized that her friend wasn't kidding about now being one of the initiates, she'd been thrilled to death. They were all going to be initiated together after all. It was so exciting.

Well, maybe not together, she reminded herself. She stole a glance at Kate. If Kate was set on joining the Coven of the Green Wood, they still wouldn't all be together. While Annie liked the coven, she was fairly sure that it wasn't the place for her. She also couldn't imagine Cooper there, which meant that Kate would be the only one of them to join it. Thinking about that made Annie a little sad, but it wasn't her biggest problem at the moment. Even more disconcerting than the idea that she might not be in the same coven with either of her friends was the fact that she wasn't sure what coven she *would* be in. She'd been doing a lot of thinking about that, and the fact was that none of the covens she'd heard about seemed right for her. The one that appealed to her most was the Daughters of the Cauldron, and she had sort of settled on them as her fallback choice in case she really couldn't decide.

I can't believe you have a safety coven, she told herself. She'd been trying not to look at it that way, but when she was honest with herself she knew it was true.

Still, there were two more covens for them to hear about that evening. *One of them will be the one*, Annie told herself. *I'm sure of it*. She decided to push her fears to the back of her mind and trust that everything would work out fine.

"We have a lot to do tonight," Sophia said to them. "After you hear from our last two presenters, you'll be asked to think about which of the covens you're interested in. Each of you will then speak to the representative of the coven you've chosen and discuss the possibility of initiation. It's a big night, so let's get started. Our first presenter is a very dear, very *old* friend of mine. His name is Owen."

A man with short brown hair and an equally short beard walked to the front of the class. "I don't know that I like that *old* part," he said, smiling.

He seems nice, Annie thought, looking at the man. She realized she was looking for a reason—any reason—to like Owen and, by extension, his coven. Still, she couldn't help it. She was feeling pressure to choose a coven, and there were only two possible candidates left before she had to go with the Daughters of the Cauldron.

"My coven is called the Starhaven Coven," Owen said. "We're a Gardnerian coven. As most of you probably know, the Gardnerian tradition of witchcraft is named after Gerald Gardner. Gardner is generally credited with revitalizing the Wiccan movement and establishing many of the rituals and invocations and chants in use by a lot of covens today. So what is a Gardnerian coven, you might ask? I'll start by saying that it's a fairly formal style of Wicca."

Sophia gave a little laugh, making her cover her mouth and causing Owen to look at her in mock annoyance.

"Okay," he said. "Compared to Sophia's style of practicing, it's *extremely* formal. We tend to use the same chants and invocations at each ritual. There's a set order to our rituals, which we follow very closely. We also have a strict hierarchy within the coven. Initiates go through three different levels of initiation, each one lasting for a fairly long period of time."

Owen paused, seeming to consider what he was telling them. "Wow," he said. "When I put it all into words it sounds sort of like joining the army or something."

The class members laughed. Owen smiled. "It's really not like that at all," he said. "But it definitely is a form of Wicca most suited to those who like order and systems."

I like those things, Annie told herself. *It sounds sort of scientific.* She knew about Gardnerian witchcraft from her reading. It was one of the most popular forms of Wicca, and there were numerous covens all over the world that owed their beginnings to Gerald Gardner. *Maybe it would work for me*, Annie thought.

"One more important thing," Owen said. "In our coven we work in partnerships. We believe in the polarity of the sexes, and whenever possible we try to pair up our male and female members. We think it makes the magical work we do stronger because it brings opposing energies together. Now, your partner doesn't have to be your actual partner. It doesn't have to be a wife or husband, or even someone you're in a romantic relationship with. But it does have to be someone you can work closely with and be comfortable with."

"What if you don't have a partner?" asked Laura.

"We prefer new members to enter the coven with partners," Owen said. "So it *is* best if you have a classmate of the opposite sex you can join with."

So much for that, Annie thought. Although she liked the guys in the class, there were none that she wanted to partner with for magical work, at least not in a one-on-one setting. Also, when she thought about it, she really liked working with many different people. And she wasn't sure she agreed that combining female and male energies made magic any more strong. She had accomplished amazing things with all kinds of combinations of people, and she didn't like the idea of restricting herself to one working partnership.

One down, one to go, she thought grimly as Owen returned to his seat at the back of the room. *This had better be it.*

Sophia appeared before them once more. "And now for something completely different," she said. "Our final presenter is also a great friend of mine, although not *quite* as old as Owen is."

Owen hissed at Sophia jokingly. "Watch out," he said. "Or I'll tell them how old you really are!"

"Forty-five next month!" Sophia shot back. "And I want presents!" Then she got back to business. "Anyway, our last presenter is Hunter. I'll let him explain what his coven is all about."

Annie found herself immediately intrigued by the last presenter. He was a young man, perhaps in his early twenties. He was tall, with long dark blond hair that was tied in a ponytail. He was wearing a T-shirt with a Celtic knot design on it, and Annie noticed he had a similar design tattooed around his right arm.

"I'm Hunter," he said. "I'm a student at Jasper College, where I major in English. I'm also the head of the student pagan group there."

I didn't even know they had one, Annie thought.

"There's a large student group at Jasper," Hunter continued. "We hold open rituals and monthly moon gatherings. But we aren't a coven. We're just a group of people interested in exploring pagan spirituality. However, I also belong to a real coven." He smiled, as if saying that his coven was real somehow made the student group nothing but a big game. "That didn't come out quite right," he said. "What I meant to say is that I also belong to a smaller coven apart from the student group. How was that?"

Annie laughed. Hunter had an easy way of speaking. He seemed relaxed and comfortable talking about Wicca. *It would be interesting being in a coven with him*, Annie found herself thinking.

"We call ourselves the Children of the Goddess," said Hunter. "We're a very diverse group, and because we're mostly college students, we're a young group."

Sounds good to me, Annie thought.

"We meet pretty regularly throughout the year," he told them. "But obviously we take breaks when school is out."

Maybe it's not so good, Annie thought, changing her mind. School was out at times when her favorite sabbats—like Midsummer and Yule—occurred. She didn't want to miss those things. So although she found Hunter interesting, and although she liked the idea of being in a coven with people close to her own age, she didn't think his coven was right for her after all.

Hunter told them a little more about the Children of the Goddess, but Annie had already decided that the group wouldn't provide her with what she needed. So when Hunter thanked them for listening to him and returned to his seat, Annie felt the knot that had been forming in her stomach solidify. The presentations were over, and she still didn't have a definite winner.

"You've now heard from five different covens," Sophia told them. She counted them off one by one. "The Daughters of the Cauldron, the Coven of the Green Wood, Freya's Circle, Starhaven Coven, and the Children of the Goddess. Five different covens with five different approaches to working magic. Think about what you've heard and about which of these covens might be right for you. The representatives are all here tonight, ready to answer any questions you might have. Feel free to come speak with us. And when you know which coven you feel drawn to, tell that coven's representative and the two of you can talk more about initiation."

The eight initiates looked around at one another. Annie knew they were all wondering what the other seven were going to do. Would they all be interested in the same few covens, or would they each pick something different? With eight of them and only five covens, there was going to have to be some overlapping. But in all likelihood they wouldn't all pick the same one.

Annie watched as her classmates stood up and began moving around. She kept a particularly careful eye on Cooper and Kate. Where would her friends go? Would she be with them or not? She already knew that Kate was likely to join the Coven of the Green Wood, and in fact after putting her cushion away that's exactly where Kate headed. Thatcher greeted her warmly, and the two of them began talking.

"How are you going to pick?" Annie asked Cooper. "You didn't get to hear all of the presentations."

As if hearing Annie's question, Sophia appeared at their side. "Cooper," she said. "Since you missed the earlier presentations, why don't you use this class to talk to the different coven reps? Then you can make your decision in the next few days."

Cooper nodded. "Sounds good to me," she said.

Sophia looked at Annie. "And what about you?" she asked.

Annie smiled nervously. "Oh, I'm giving it all a lot of thought," she said.

Sophia nodded and returned to the other reps. Shortly after, Ben went over to speak with her, and she turned her attention to him.

"I'm going to go talk to that woman from the

Norse coven," Cooper told Annie. "Have fun."

"Sure," Annie said.

She wished Cooper hadn't left her alone. That made her feel conspicuous. Everyone else was speaking with coven representatives. Ben was still conversing with Sophia. Cooper was talking to Polly. Thatcher was standing with Kate, and they had been joined by Emma. Ben was talking to Hunter from the Children of the Goddess, while Roger and Laura were having an animated discussion with Owen from Starhaven Coven. Ezra was walking from one group to the next, listening for a moment before moving on.

What are they all thinking? wondered Annie. *Do they all know for certain where they belong?* It bothered her that no one coven seemed to call to her. She knew which ones she *wouldn't* be happy in, and that was a start. But choosing the Daughters of the Cauldron simply because it was *okay* didn't make her happy. She wanted to be absolutely certain of her choice.

She felt stupid just standing there, so eventually she wandered over to listen to what people were saying. Mostly the representatives were just holding casual conversations with the people gathered around them. It seemed that, indeed, most of her classmates had made up their minds. Even Ezra seemed to have settled on one coven, chatting happily with Polly. Cooper had finished her conversation and came to stand by Annie.

"Made up your mind?" she asked Annie.

"I think so," Annie answered, trying to sound sure of herself. "You?"

"Almost," Cooper told her. "I'm going to think about it for a couple of days."

"Okay," Sophia called out. "It looks as if you've mostly made up your minds. Why don't you all go to your final choices now."

Annie's classmates all remained where they were standing. They looked around at one another, seeing who had selected which group. They all seemed very happy. Even Hunter, who didn't have a single person in his group, looked around with a pleased expression. Only Annie wasn't standing anywhere in particular.

For a moment she almost went to stand with Hunter because she felt sorry for him. But she knew that would be a *really* dumb way to pick a coven. Still, she had to choose, and fast. People were beginning to notice that she hadn't gone to any representative. She could only pretend that she was standing with Cooper for so long.

Finally she made her move and went to stand by Sophia. Her teacher smiled at her and gave her a hug. Annie smiled back. *Maybe this is where I'm meant to be after all*, she told herself. *Maybe I was just afraid to make that commitment.* Now that she had chosen, and was standing next to Sophia and Ben, she really did feel better. She looked at Kate, standing beside Thatcher, and gave her a smile. She was going to miss working magic with her friend, but perhaps going their separate ways was all part of maturing and becoming the witches they were meant to be.

"It seems everyone has chosen," said Sophia. She looked at Cooper. "All except one. But she'll choose in the next day or two. Representatives, if you're happy with your initiates, then our work here is done."

The five representatives looked at the students gathered around them. Everyone appeared delighted with the way things had worked out. Sophia nodded. "The representatives will now discuss the details of their initiations with their students," she said. "As I told you at the start of this initiatory period, each group will perform its own initiations. We've decided, however, that all of us will meet together after those initiations to welcome the new witches into their larger community. So while tonight is the last time you'll see most of your fellow students as dedicants, you'll all have your graduation of sorts on the thirteenth."

They broke into four groups, with Cooper and Hunter as the leftovers. The two of them sat on the couch talking while the others met with their new coven leaders. Annie and Ben sat with Sophia in one corner of the room, where she filled them in on what would happen at their initiations.

"I'm really pleased that the two of you have chosen the Daughters of the Cauldron," she said, sounding genuinely excited. "Ben because we could use some male energy in the group and Annie because you remind me so much of myself when I was your age."

Really? Annie thought, pleased by the compliment. More and more she was deciding that she really had chosen correctly in picking Sophia's coven. Although the knot in her stomach was still there, she was sure now that it was just the remnants of her nervousness over the night's proceedings.

"I'm not going to tell you very much about your initiations," Sophia said. "All I'll say is that you need to be here at six o'clock and you should have chosen ritual names that reflect who you feel you are as witches. Those are the names you'll use in our circles."

"We can pick any names?" Ben asked.

Sophia nodded. "You can be Mighty Mouse if you want to," she said, smiling. "Anything that captures your personality."

"And that's it?" Annie said. It sounded almost too easy.

"That's all I'll *tell* you," said Sophia mysteriously.

She sat and talked with Ben and Annie while the other groups finished up. When they were done, everyone said their good-byes and Annie headed out with Cooper and Kate. Cooper had driven, so they were spared taking the bus home.

"So, what weird stuff do you guys have to do for your initiations?" Cooper asked her friends as they drove out of the downtown area.

"Just pick a ritual name," Annie said. "What about you, Kate?"

"I'm supposed to bring an object to put on the coven altar," Kate said.

Apart from that discussion, they said very little on the ride home, with each of them lost in her own thoughts. For Annie there was also an element of sadness to the ride. *This feels like the last night we'll all be together*, she thought. *Pretty soon we'll all be in different covens.*

"What are you guys doing tomorrow night?" she asked suddenly.

"No plans," said Cooper.

"None here either," added Kate.

"Can we do a full moon ritual?" asked Annie. "Just the three of us."

Cooper looked at her and gave her a smile, knowing what her friend was getting at. So did Kate. They both nodded.

"Let's do it at the beach," suggested Kate, naming the place where they'd done their first real ritual together.

"Becka and Grayson are coming tomorrow, but I can get away," Annie said.

Again silence fell, but this time it was a more comfortable, if somewhat sad, quiet. Annie felt better, though. They would have one last ritual together before their initiations. It would be a good way to close their year together.

Cooper arrived at Annie's house, where Annie got out. "See you guys at school tomorrow," she said, waving and closing the door.

When she got inside she found Aunt Sarah standing in the living room wearing her Alice outfit. Juliet was pinning the hem.

"It looks fantastic," said Annie, going in for a closer look.

"Juliet is a wonder," said Aunt Sarah.

"A wonder who needs more pins," Juliet said, standing up. "I'll be right back. They're in my room."

She disappeared up the stairs while Annie gazed at her aunt. She couldn't believe that in a few days Aunt Sarah would be married.

"How did you know Grayson was the one?" she asked, surprising herself.

Aunt Sarah smiled. "I knew because for the first time in my life I didn't feel like I was settling for something," she told her niece. "I didn't have to say 'He's really nice, but he has bad breath' or 'He's smart, but he's rude at restaurants.' I didn't have to make excuses for him."

Annie nodded. *Settling.* The word stuck in her mind. It's what she'd been worrying about all night. Was she doing that in choosing Sophia's coven? She wanted to believe that it was the right coven for her. She'd been trying to convince herself of it all night. But every time she felt she was absolutely sure of her decision, she found herself with a nagging doubt.

"Sometimes you just know," her aunt said, looking at her with a smile of pure happiness. "You just know."

Then she discontinued and looked at each of their faces, then with a new look with a small at once happening then just know

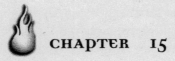

CHAPTER 15

The following night was cold and clear. It was as if winter were trying to pull back the year from spring for just one more day. The temperature had dropped, and the stars sparkled in the black sky. When Kate arrived at the cove to meet her friends, she was glad she'd put on a heavy sweater.

"Why don't we ever seem to be doing this when it's warm?" Cooper complained as the three of them got to work.

Kate made a circle of rocks in which to build a fire, while Annie went and collected some seawater in the cauldron she'd brought with her from home. Cooper picked up driftwood for the fire and brought it to the circle of stones.

"At least we've gotten more efficient at this," remarked Kate as she built up a fire using some pieces of newspaper and the smallest of the sticks. The first time she'd attempted to make a fire there, it had taken forever to get it going. This time, though, she had one crackling in a matter of minutes.

The three of them stood and faced east. As Kate gazed in the direction of the city, with its bright lights and the sounds of cars and people, she thought about how casting a circle had become so familiar to the three of them. Again she thought about their first fumbling attempts at doing it. They had all felt self-conscious, afraid of saying or doing the wrong thing. Now they did it with ease, falling comfortably into the pattern.

"East," Annie called out in her clear, confident voice. "Power of air, be with us in our circle tonight."

"South," Cooper called next as they turned to look in that direction. "Power of fire, be with us in our circle."

Kate's turn was next, and she called the west and the power of water into their circle as the three of them looked over the ocean. And then Annie finished invoking the elements by turning to look at the line of rocks through which they'd entered the cove and saying, "North, power of earth, be with us in our circle."

Having summoned the four elements of the directions, it was time to complete the circle. This fell to Cooper, who picked up a stick and pressed the end into the sand.

"In the sand I draw the circle," she said as she walked around the fire, inscribing a circle with the stick. "In the circle magic dwells. All who enter are protected, here to weave our magic spells."

She completed the circle, broke the stick in two, and added it to the fire. The three of them were standing together within the shape she had drawn. Above them, the full moon shone down with ghostly light.

"Here we are," Annie said. "Our last circle as baby witches."

Kate and Cooper laughed. To Kate it almost felt as if they were playing a game of pretend. She found it difficult to really believe that in just over a week they would all be initiated. Had it really been a year? She thought back to the first time she, Cooper, and Annie had gathered on that same beach. In some ways the time had gone more quickly than she ever could have imagined, while in others it seemed like a lifetime ago.

"I decided which coven I want to join," Cooper said. She paused as the others looked at her, waiting for an answer. "I'm going with the Children of the Goddess," she said.

"Really?" Kate said, surprised. She had been expecting Cooper, like Annie, to join Sophia's coven.

"I know," Cooper said. "I was a little surprised myself. But while you guys were all talking, I had a really good time talking to Hunter. It sounds like the people in his coven are into a lot of the same things I am. I thought about it last night and all day today, and I called him just before I came here. I think it will be a good place for me."

"Wow," Annie said. "We each picked a different coven."

"Well, we always were really different people," remarked Kate. She knew Annie was a little upset that they wouldn't all be together, and she wanted to try to make her feel better. "Maybe it makes sense that we're all in different covens."

Annie nodded. "I guess it couldn't last forever," she said.

"What shall we do on our last big blow-out?" asked Cooper.

Annie indicated the cauldron of seawater that she'd placed inside the circle. It was sitting directly in a spot of moonlight and the water within it glistened with the reflection of the pearly orb hanging over their heads.

"Seawater touched by the moon is supposed to have all kinds of magical properties," she said. She reached into the pocket of the coat she was wearing and brought out three small glass bottles. "I thought we could charge the water with our intentions and put it in these bottles. Then we can each have one on our altars. That way we'll always have a piece of the magic we created together."

The three of them knelt in the sand with the cauldron between them. They joined hands, encircling the pot of seawater.

"How do you want to charge it?" Cooper asked Annie.

"Using one of the ways we first used to raise energy," said Annie. "I want to do a word chain."

The others nodded. Making a word chain was, like

casting a circle, old hat for them by now. They'd done it often, and they knew it was a good way to focus their energy and create power for their magical work.

"Ending," Annie said, starting the chain.

"Beginning," said Cooper.

"Change," Kate said, letting the first word that came to her mind be the one she spoke.

Annie followed her with, "Transform," with Cooper adding, "Grow."

"Blossom," said Kate, imagining a seed bursting open and the plant inside reaching out.

Around they went, forming the chain word by word, link by link. As each girl's word caused the next one to think of something else, they moved faster and faster, their voices blending smoothly into a river of sound. Kate listened, the words bringing images to life in her mind.

"Leaf." "Tree." "Forest." "Path." "Walk." "Journey," they said as Kate imagined herself traveling down a narrow path that wound between tall pine trees.

"Travel." "Adventure." "Search." The words reminded Kate of the year they'd just spent exploring the ways of Wicca, taking a journey into themselves and seeing what they found there.

"Home." "Friends." "Love." The last word was Kate's. She pictured herself arriving home after a long trip, being welcomed by the people who loved her. And when she looked at the faces of the people who held their arms out to her in her vision, they were the faces of Annie and Cooper.

The chain was complete. They didn't add to it. Instead they sat around the cauldron, still holding hands, not speaking. Kate imagined the cauldron swirling with golden light, the power of their intentions turning it into a whirlpool of energy. She knew that the others had done the same thing, and that what had moments ago been ordinary seawater was now something else.

Reluctantly, Kate let her friends' hands slip from hers as Annie reached for the bottles she'd brought. She handed one each to Kate and Cooper. Then the three of them dipped their hands into the cauldron, letting the water fill the bottles. When they lifted them out again, they held them up to the moon. The water inside sparkled brightly.

"We all come from the Goddess," Annie sang.

"And to her we shall return," Cooper and Kate sang, joining her. "Like a drop of rain flowing to the ocean."

It was the first song they had learned, and it seemed particularly appropriate to Kate for their final full moon ritual together. Like the drops of rain, they too returned again and again to the ocean to celebrate their connection to the Goddess and to one another. Now they each had some of that magic bottled up, ready to be placed on their altars, where it would always remind them of how it had all begun.

The three of them clicked their bottles together as if they were toasting the moon, the Goddess, and each other. Then they lowered their hands and sat with the bottles cradled in their laps.

"And so it ends," Annie said.

"You make it sound so dramatic," Kate told her. "It's not like we'll never work together again or anything."

Annie sighed. "I know," she said. "But it will be different. It won't be like this."

Kate looked down at the bottle in her hand. She knew that Annie was right. It *would* be different. Soon they would all be celebrating their rituals with different people. Sure, they would come together with their friends for certain occasions, but for the most part their magical work would be done with their new witch families. But wasn't that all part of the journey, too? They had started out together, supported one another along the way. Now it was time for each of them to step out on her own.

Kate really believed that. At least she *wanted* to believe that. But when she allowed her real feelings to come out, she had to admit that she was sad about not being with Cooper and Annie anymore. She reached out for Annie's hand. Annie took it, and Kate held out her other hand to Cooper, who did the same thing.

"What do we always say when we open a circle?" she asked them.

"The circle is open," Cooper said, repeating the

first part of the familiar closing line of the ritual.

"But unbroken," concluded Annie.

"Right," Kate said. "And that's how it is with us. Our circle is always going to be unbroken, even if we're in different covens, even if someday we're living far apart and don't see each other like we do now. No one can take away what we've done together this past year. We're always going to be a circle of three."

"You're right," Annie said. Kate could see that she was blinking back tears, and that made her want to cry, too.

"Besides," Cooper said, "no one said we can't sneak away for our very own rituals every now and again."

Annie gave a combination laugh and sniffle. "I think that's against the rules or something," she said.

"Rules," Cooper said, as if the very word tasted awful. "Haven't we taught you that breaking the rules can be *fun*?"

"That and about fifty other things that could land me in jail," Annie replied.

"We're all going to be fine," said Kate. "Just think of it as starting at a new school or something like that."

"That's not exactly a comforting analogy," Annie told her friend. "But I get the point."

They sat for a few more minutes, still holding hands and not speaking. They looked into the flames of the fire, which was dying down. Kate felt the cold wind blow on the back of her neck where it faced the sea, and she shivered. It was time to end the circle.

"Merry meet," she said, giving Annie's hand a squeeze.

"Merry part," Annie said, squeezing Cooper's.

"And merry meet again," Cooper finished, completing the circle with a squeeze of Kate's hand.

They released each other's hands and stood up. Annie dumped the remaining seawater in the cauldron onto the fire, and it went out with a hiss. Cooper stirred the sodden ashes with a stick, making sure the fire was completely out.

"Shall we rub the circle out?" Kate asked, looking at the design Cooper had etched in the sand. They usually removed all traces of their activities when they were done.

"No," Cooper said. "Let's leave this one."

"If the Goddess wants it gone she'll send a particularly high tide," said Annie thoughtfully.

The three of them gathered up their things and left the cove, not looking back. They walked across the beach to the long set of wooden stairs that led to the wharf, and climbed them slowly. When they reached the top Cooper said, "Who wants a ride?"

"I'll take one," Annie said. "I left Becka getting fitted for her Cheshire Cat costume. I'm sure she's going crazy."

"I actually drove myself," Kate said. "My father

let me use his car. I'll see you guys tomorrow."

Annie and Cooper each hugged her and then walked away. Kate went in the other direction, having found a parking space nearby. When she reached her car she got in, started it up, and pulled out of the spot. It felt odd driving herself home. She was so used to taking the bus or just sitting as a passenger in someone else's car. Driving made it a new experience.

As she made her way through town she reflected on the ritual she'd just done with her friends. She'd tried hard to comfort Annie, who seemed to be taking the dissolution of their group the hardest. But really she'd been trying to comfort herself. Although she didn't want her friends to know, she was terrified about what was in store for her. Everything that had become so familiar to her was being taken away, and she wished she had something to hold on to, something that would keep her connected to the things she was used to.

Like an old blanket, she thought. *Or an old boyfriend*. The thought popped into her head totally without warning. It hit her so hard that for a moment she was unable to move. When she realized that she was still driving, she forced herself to put her foot on the brake. A car behind her honked loudly, but she ignored it, pulling over to the side and coming to a stop.

An old boyfriend, she thought again. *An old boyfriend is like an old security blanket. They're both familiar. How* many times had she seen friends of hers do the same thing—run back to old boyfriends because they provided a sense of security, even though they were almost certain to do the things again that had made them ex-boyfriends in the first place.

"That's what you're doing," she said aloud. "You're going back to Tyler because you don't want to be hurt by your circle breaking up, not because you really want to be with him."

She couldn't believe that she hadn't realized what was going on. She'd convinced herself that although she'd sworn never to go out with Tyler again, she'd been mistaken. She'd convinced herself that she owed it to him—and to herself—to give him another chance. But really what she'd been doing was trying to give herself a safety net, something to catch her when the security of her circle was taken away from her.

No wonder I kept having doubts, she thought. *Deep down I knew that the Coven of the Green Wood wasn't right for me*. Now that she was able to give voice to her fear, she knew it was true. The Coven of the Green Wood *wasn't* right for her. It was simply the safest place for her, and that was very different. Yet somehow she'd convinced herself that she was doing the right thing.

At first she was relieved to have figured out what was bothering her. Then, just as suddenly as it had come, the good feeling went away. She had figured out her mistake, but now she was going to have to correct it. And that meant doing two things. First, she had to tell Tyler that she wouldn't go to the movies—or on any other kind of date—with him. Second—and even harder—she was going to have to tell the Coven of the Green Wood that she'd changed her mind.

"Now where am I going to go?" she asked herself. If she gave up her coven, she would have to find another one. But where else would she fit in? Who else would have her? She didn't have the slightest idea. Sitting in her car, with her friends driving home together while she tried to figure out what to do next, she suddenly felt very much alone.

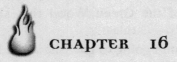

CHAPTER 16

Cooper stared at the phone, willing it to ring. It was Thursday afternoon. She'd gotten home from school half an hour earlier and found a message for her on the answering machine—a message from Betty Bangs's manager. Cooper had been so excited that she'd played it six times.

"This message is for Cooper Rivers. This is Serena Mao returning your call from Monday. I spoke with Betty, and she confirmed that she would like the Bitter Pills to be part of the tour this summer. Give me a call back and we can discuss the details."

Cooper had called immediately, reaching Serena Mao's assistant. He'd told her that Serena was on the phone at the moment but would call Cooper right back. That had been ten minutes ago. To Cooper every minute seemed like an hour. She was so anxious to speak with Betty's manager that she could hardly stand it. She was pacing around her room, trying to imagine what it would be like for her and Jane to play on a stage in front of thousands of people. *Well, hundreds at least,* she told herself.

When the phone finally rang, Cooper practically threw it across the room in her haste to answer it.

"Hello," she said breathlessly.

"Cooper?"

It wasn't Serena Mao. It was Cooper's father. She hadn't spoken to him since the incident with Amanda Barclay almost two weeks before. He'd left half a dozen messages, but each time Cooper had either found excuses for not calling him back or left perfunctory messages on his answering machine when she knew he wouldn't be at home. Now she was tempted to just hang up, but she knew she couldn't do that.

"Hi," she said. "Um, this really isn't a good time." She didn't want to be on the phone in case Serena Mao called back.

"You can't avoid me forever, Cooper," Mr. Rivers said, sounding hurt. "We have to talk about what happened."

"I know," Cooper said. "But not now. I'm kind of expecting an important call."

"I see," her father replied. "And I'm not important?"

"No," Cooper said. "I mean yes, you're important. But this is a business call."

"Cooper, I know you're upset about my seeing Amanda—" her father began.

Just then the call waiting alert sounded. Cooper groaned. "Dad, I have to go," she said. "I'll call you back, I promise."

Before her father could say anything Cooper switched to the second call. This time it really was Serena Mao.

"Betty was very insistent that we sign you to this tour," she told Cooper after they'd exchanged greetings.

"I still can't quite believe it," Cooper told her. "It's like a dream come true for Jane and me."

Again the call waiting clicked in. Cooper was hesitant to ask Serena Mao to hold, but she was afraid it might be something important.

"Can you hang on for just a second?" Cooper asked, feeling like an idiot.

"No problem," Serena told her.

Cooper clicked over. "Hello?"

"I don't like being hung up on." Her father sounded angry.

"Dad, I *have* to talk to this woman. I said I'd call you back."

"What is so important that you can't talk to me for a minute?" her father asked.

Cooper gave a sigh of irritation. Why was her father choosing this particular moment to throw a tantrum? "Look," she said. "I have got to go. I *promise* I will call you back."

"No," Mr. Rivers said. "Meet me for dinner tonight."

"Fine," Cooper said. "Where?"

"My apartment. Six o'clock."

"Okay," Cooper said. "Now good-bye."

Again she hung up. "I'm really sorry about that," she told Serena Mao. "Parent trauma."

Serena laughed. "You know, when I got involved in the music business I never thought that one of the things I'd have to deal with would be parents. But the acts keep getting younger and younger. Last week one of my artists had to cancel a gig because her mother didn't want her out past ten o'clock. I tell you, sometimes I feel like a baby-sitter."

"Oh, it gets worse," Cooper told her. "My dad's a lawyer."

Serena gave a little moan. "The worst," she said. "He's not going to give us any trouble about your joining the tour for a few weeks is he?"

Cooper thought about the bad mood her father was currently in. At the moment she didn't think he'd even agree to let her *go* to a concert, let alone perform at one. *You're going to have to be really nice to him*, she told herself.

"He'll be fine," she told Serena.

"Good," Serena said. "Since you and Jane aren't eighteen yet, we're going to need parental permission for you to be on the tour. But don't worry. I'll talk to them and explain how it all works. I'm pretty good at calming parents down. Besides, these tours aren't like they used to be. Every so often someone throws a TV out a hotel window or something, but you're more likely to find the bands doing yoga and meditating than partying all night."

"My mother will be thrilled to hear that," Cooper said.

"Well, if everything works out we'd like the Bitter Pills to play about a dozen dates on the West Coast leg of the tour," Serena told her. "You'd get a thirty-minute set on the second stage during prime time. It's not the main stage, but let me tell you, I've seen a lot of acts get signed from the second stage. Record company scouts love to discover new talent there, and you never know who's going to be in the crowd."

Cooper hadn't even thought about the possibility that she and Jane might be seen by record company people. She'd been excited enough just at the prospect of playing live as part of a rock tour. The thought of maybe being discovered was almost too much to consider.

"Have you thought about getting a manager?" Serena asked her.

"Um, no," Cooper said. "I mean, we've only really played at local clubs."

"Well, you should have one just in case," Serena told her. "If you do get offers, you'll need someone to handle them."

"Okay," Cooper said, feeling a little stunned at how quickly things were happening. She heard someone speaking to Serena on the other end.

"I have to go," Serena told her. "Have your parents call me. Jane's, too. Maybe we can all get together and talk about the tour. In the mean-time, think about getting that manager."

"I will," Cooper said. "And I'll have my parents call you right away. Bye."

She hung up. Her heart was racing and she thought she might pass out from sheer happiness. It was really happening—she and Jane were going to be part of Betty Bangs's tour. She needed to tell someone. She needed to tell *everyone*. But the first person she needed to tell was Jane herself. She picked up the phone and called her.

"We're doing it," she said as soon as Jane picked up. "We're on the tour."

She had to hold the phone away from her ear while Jane screamed. Jane, when she had calmed down enough to talk, said, "Please tell me you're not kidding."

"I'm not kidding," Cooper said. "I just got off the phone with Serena Mao. As long as our parents agree, we're in. Twelve dates. Thirty minutes." She hesitated about telling Jane what else Serena had said, but finally she said, "Possible record contract."

Again she had to hold the phone away from her ear while Jane yelled. Jane came back on and said, "I have to go. My mother is convinced I'm having a nervous breakdown. I'll call you later. This is *so* cool."

Cooper hung up. Jane was right—it was cool. She picked up the phone again, and this time she dialed T.J.'s number. When he answered she told him every single word of her conversation with Betty's manager.

"And she's so nice," Cooper concluded.

"Wow," T.J. said. "I can't believe it. My girl-friend is going to be a rock star. Hey, if this works out you won't have to worry about where you're going to college. You'll be too busy doing inter-views with Carson Daly on *TRL*."

"Right," Cooper said, snorting. But then she thought about it. What if T.J. was right? What if Serena was right, and a record company did sign her and Jane? What would it mean? The idea was so overwhelming that she pushed it to the back of her mind.

"It looks like quitting Schroedinger's Cat was the best decision you ever made," T.J. said.

"What do you mean?" asked Cooper.

"Well, if you hadn't quit you would never have met Jane," he said. "And if you'd never met Jane you would never have formed the Bitter Pills. It's all a big chain of events, you know."

Cooper thought about that. T.J. was right, but only sort of. He hadn't followed the chain of events back far enough. Yes, quitting Schroedinger's Cat had been an important step, but she never would have quit the band if the other members hadn't objected to performing her Wiccan-themed songs. And she never would have written those songs if she hadn't gotten involved in witchcraft to begin with.

So, really, it could all be attributed to the fact that she'd decided to study the Craft. *One more good thing that's come out of it,* she thought happily.

"I'm really happy for you," T.J. said. "You just have to promise me that when you get big you'll let Schroedinger's Cat open up for you on your tour."

Cooper laughed. "How about this," she said, "you can be our main groupie."

"Only if I get to throw my underwear onstage," T.J. answered.

"Deal," said Cooper. "Look, I have to go. How about we do something tomorrow night?"

"Blowing me off already?" T.J. said, pretending to be hurt.

"I have to have dinner with my dad," Cooper told him. "It's time to deal with the Amanda Barclay thing."

"That should be fun," T.J. said. "Call me later if you want and let me know how it goes."

Cooper hung up. There were other people she wanted to call—Kate and Annie in particular—but she had to get ready for dinner with her father. Plus, she heard her mother come into the house, and she wanted to tell her the good news. She was pretty sure she could get her mother to agree to let her go on the tour, but she had to handle it carefully. So before she left her room she took a minute to calm herself. Then she said a little prayer to the Goddess asking for help, and went downstairs.

An hour later she left the house in high sprits. Talking to her mother had been easier than she'd anticipated. Her mother had been very excited for her, and to Cooper's amazement she'd said that as long as Mr. Rivers agreed that it was okay, and as long as Serena Mao answered a few remaining questions, Cooper had her permission to play the tour. Cooper had been so thrilled that she'd given her mother a big hug and a kiss, something she rarely did.

Now I just have to get Dad to say okay, she told herself as she drove to his apartment for dinner. Normally that would be no problem. But given that she and her father hadn't exactly been the best of friends recently, she wasn't sure how he would take her news and request for permission.

She reached his building and parked. The front desk attendant called up to her father's apartment to announce her arrival and Cooper got into the elevator. She'd only been to her father's apartment on a few occasions, and never for dinner. As she rode the elevator to the nineteenth floor, she found herself wondering why he'd chosen to eat in instead of going to a restaurant. He wasn't a particularly good cook, and Cooper wasn't even sure he'd ever used the kitchen in his apartment. The few times she'd been there the only things in his refrigerator had been a couple of limes and a container of vanilla ice cream.

When the elevator stopped she got out and walked to her father's door. Pausing a moment, she rang the bell and waited. A moment later her father answered.

"Hi," Cooper said.

Her father gave her a quick hug and showed her in, shutting the door behind her. Cooper made a quick scan of the apartment.

"You got furniture," she said, noticing a new couch and chairs and some other pieces she'd never seen before.

"Yeah," her father said. "Amanda helped me pick some things out."

Cooper felt a chill descend upon her at the mention of Amanda Barclay's name. She'd been hoping that the dinner invitation didn't include having to see Amanda again. Now she assumed that it would.

"Don't worry," her father said. "She's not joining us tonight."

Cooper relaxed a little. Not having to deal with Amanda Barclay was one less thing to worry about.

"Shall we eat?" her father asked her.

"Sure," said Cooper, still curious about what they were having. The dining table was set with plates and silverware, but Cooper couldn't smell anything cooking.

"Sit down," Mr. Rivers said. "I'll bring the food."

Cooper sat down. A moment later her father came out carrying a big brown shopping bag. He placed it on the table and started lifting containers out.

"Since you missed dinner at Shiva's Garden

last time, I thought I'd give you a second chance," he said as he opened the containers and revealed several different Indian dishes. Then he took the seat across from Cooper. "I figured if I did takeout you couldn't run out on me," he said.

Cooper rolled her eyes. "I'm sorry about that," she said, spooning some vegetable curry onto her plate. "I just couldn't sit across from her and eat at the same time."

Her father gave her a look. "Her name is Amanda," he said. "And I happen to like her."

Cooper wasn't sure how to respond. The only things she could think of to say about Amanda Barclay were all negative, and she didn't want to hurt her father's feelings by saying them. Even more, she didn't want to make him angry. She still had to tell him about Betty Bangs and the opportunity the Bitter Pills had to play on her tour.

"Cooper, I know you've had some run-ins with Amanda in the past. And yes, I think she made some mistakes. But she's not a bad person."

Cooper simply smiled as she ate some lemon dal. *Just keep stuffing your mouth and you won't have to talk*, she told herself.

"You just have to get to know her," her father continued. "You actually have a lot of the same interests. For instance, she's really into music."

Here's your chance, Cooper thought. "Speaking of music," she said, "I have something to ask you."

She told her father about meeting Betty Bangs

and about being offered a spot on the tour she was putting together. "It's a really wonderful opportunity," she said, trying to sound enthusiastic. "And Mom said it's okay with her if it's okay with you."

She paused, watching her father's face for some indication of what he was thinking. He chewed silently for a minute, as if his brain was processing the information he'd been given. With each passing second Cooper grew more and more tense. If he said no, she knew she would die on the spot.

"Tell you what," Mr. Rivers said finally, wiping his mouth on his napkin. "I'll make you a deal."

"Yeah?" Cooper said warily. Her father was, after all, a lawyer, and she'd heard him use that same tone of voice with clients.

"You can do it," he said, making Cooper want to jump up in excitement. "On two conditions."

"What are they?" Cooper asked.

"First, I get to be your manager," her father said.

Cooper thought about that. Maybe her father's lawyer skills would come in handy after all. "Okay," she said. "I have to ask Jane, but I think it will be okay."

Her father nodded. "And second, you have to be nice to Amanda."

Cooper rolled her eyes.

"I'm serious," her father said. "You have to be nice. And not just polite. You have to actually *talk* to her and go places with us."

Cooper looked at him. It was time to negotiate.

"I'll agree to *one* conversation and *two* outings to be named later."

"*Three* conversations and *five* outings," said Mr. Rivers. "All within a two-month period."

"*Two* conversations and *three* outings," countered Cooper.

Her father regarded her for a moment. "Done," he said, reaching across the table and shaking her hand.

"Nice doing business with you," said Cooper.

They both laughed.

"Now let's talk about college," Mr. Rivers said.

"Don't push your luck," Cooper said. "It's your girlfriend *or* college, but not both."

CHAPTER 17

"This has got to be the most fabulous tail ever," Becka told Juliet. She was standing in front of the mirror in Annie's bedroom, admiring the costume she'd just put on. Juliet had finished it just that afternoon, and they'd been waiting for Annie to get home from school to show it to her.

"Don't you love it, Annie?" Becka asked, twirling the tail around and cocking her head to look at the ears Juliet had made and attached to a plastic headband.

"Annie?" Juliet said when her sister didn't respond.

"Oh," Annie said, as if they'd startled her. "Yeah, it's really cool."

Juliet looked at Becka, and the two of them eyed Annie.

"What gives?" Becka asked. "You're totally preoccupied."

Annie made a gesture of dismissal. "It's not important," she said.

"It is if it means you're not paying attention to my fabulous costumes!" exclaimed Juliet.

Annie sighed. "Well, I was sort of thinking about something. But I don't want to bother you guys."

"Bother," Becka said, sitting on the edge of Annie's bed.

"Yeah," Juliet said, sitting on the other side of her. "Spill it."

"It's this whole initiation thing," said Annie. "I'm having some doubts about it."

"You don't want to be initiated?" asked Juliet. "I thought you were really looking forward to it."

"Oh, I am," said Annie. "I still want to be initiated. I'm just not sure I picked the right coven."

"Not that I'm an expert on covens or anything," said Becka, "but is there one you like better or something?"

Annie shook her head. "That's just it," she replied. "I think I picked the best one. But I'm not sure it's the *right* one."

Juliet nodded. "I get it," she said. "You chose it because it was the least wrong, not because it was the most right."

"Yes," Annie said. "I mean, I had to pick one, so I picked the one that seemed to make the most sense."

Juliet laughed. "I can't tell you how many times I've done that with boyfriends," she said.

"Amen," said Becka, giving Juliet a high five over Annie's head.

"So how did you fix it?" asked Annie.

"Dumped them," Juliet said simply.

"That's all you *can* do," Becka said, rubbing her face with one of the soft purple-and-pink gloves Juliet had created to look like paws. "Otherwise you just sit around hoping it will eventually feel right."

"And it never does," said Juliet. "Trust me on this, your first instinct is always right. If something feels wrong, chances are pretty high that it is."

"That's what I was afraid of," said Annie glumly. She threw herself back on the bed and groaned. "What am I going to do?"

"Isn't there some kind of ritual you could do to get some advice?" asked Juliet. "I don't know, Tarot cards or something like that."

"I did the cards yesterday," Annie replied. "They weren't any help. All I got out of them was that I was going to have to make a choice and that some big change would come from it. Like I didn't know that already."

"What about talking to someone?" Becka suggested. "I mean besides us. Isn't there someone you can ask for help?"

"Normally I'd say yes," Annie said, thinking of Sophia and Archer. They had often helped her out with her problems. "But they're sort of part of the problem," she told Becka.

"I think that pretty much wears out my suggestions," Becka told her. "Sorry."

"What you need is a Caterpillar," said Juliet thoughtfully.

"What?" Annie said.

"A Caterpillar," repeated Juliet. "You know, like the one Alice asked for advice. He was very helpful."

Annie laughed. "Yeah, but *I'm* supposed to be the Caterpillar, remember? I can't very well ask myself for advice. I'm the one who got me into this situation in the first place."

She sat up again and stared at the wall, thinking. It *would* have helped if she'd had a Caterpillar to go to, someone who could give her a push in the right direction. But she wasn't in Wonderland, and there was no Caterpillar to be found.

Then an image popped into her mind—the image of a face. It didn't belong to a Caterpillar, but it belonged to someone almost as mysterious.

"Eulalie," Annie said.

"Who?" asked Becka.

"Eulalie," Annie repeated. "She's a friend of mine. I need to go see her."

She got up and grabbed her coat from the chair. "I'll be back in a little while," she said.

"Where are you going?" asked Juliet.

Annie grinned. "Down the rabbit hole," she said as she left the room.

She asked her aunt if she could borrow the car for an errand. Aunt Sarah was so frazzled with trying to organize all the last-minute details of the wedding that she simply tossed her niece the car keys and mumbled something unintelligible. Before she could realize what Annie had asked, Annie ran out of the house and got in the car.

Fifteen minutes later she drove into the parking lot of Shady Hills, the nursing home where she had been a volunteer for a time. Getting out of the car, she walked up the sidewalk to the front door and went inside. A few minutes later she was standing outside the room of Eulalie Parsons.

"Knock, knock," she said, peering inside.

Eulalie was sitting in her favorite chair, reading a book. She didn't even look up when Annie spoke to her, she simply said, "'Bout time you got here. I was expecting you two days ago."

Annie laughed. She entered the room and approached Eulalie, who put down her book and looked up, smiling. Annie leaned down and gave the old woman a big hug and a kiss.

"I'm sorry I've been so bad about coming to see you," said Annie. "Things have been really crazy lately."

"Like they're not exciting around here?" asked Eulalie, looking at Annie sternly. "Why, just last week Annabelle Morrow lost her false teeth and it took three volunteers to find them."

"Wow," Annie said, pretending to be impressed. "That *is* something. I don't know how you get any sleep with all that carrying-on."

Eulalie cackled. "Sit down," she said. "Tell me why you came."

Annie perched on the edge of Eulalie's bed and folded her hands in her lap. "I need some advice," she said.

"Good thing I've got some," said Eulalie.

"Wait a minute," Annie said. "If you knew I was coming, how come you don't know what I want?"

Eulalie fixed her with a stern eye. "Just because I know someone is coming don't mean I know *why*," she said. She looked up in the air above her head. "When is this child going to *learn*?" she asked.

"Still talking to Ben?" inquired Annie. Eulalie had moved into Ben Rowe's room after the old man died. That's how she and Annie had met. It had soon become clear to Annie that Eulalie had some kind of powers, and this had been confirmed when she'd caught Eulalie speaking to Ben's spirit one day.

"From time to time," Eulalie answered. "He's got some other business occupying him these days, so we don't talk as much as we used to."

"Other business," Annie repeated. She didn't ask what business Ben's ghost might have to take care of. She knew Eulalie wouldn't tell her anyway. The old woman was very secretive about her abilities, and Annie suspected she didn't know even half of what Eulalie could do if she put her mind to it. "Well, you tell him hello from me," she told her.

Eulalie nodded. "Now what about *you*?" she asked.

Annie sighed. "I'm getting initiated next week," she said. "My class is over, and it's time for us to officially become witches. We all had to pick a coven we wanted to join, and I picked one. The problem is, I don't think I picked the right one."

Eulalie listened, her dark eyes bright as she watched Annie's face. Annie knew that one of the things Eulalie could do was see energy around people. Depending on the color and shape of it, she could also often tell how that person was feeling and what kind of problem she was having. Annie wondered what Eulalie saw around her.

"No, you didn't pick the right one," Eulalie told her. "But that's because your right one wasn't offered to you."

"But I had to pick one of them," said Annie.

Eulalie nodded. "That's right," she said. "I know that. All I'm saying is that none of them would have been the right one."

"Then where does that leave me?" Annie asked, slapping her hands against her knees in frustration.

"Can't tell you that," said Eulalie.

"Can't or won't?" Annie asked her.

Eulalie smiled, her teeth flashing. "You know me too well," she said. "You're right—sometimes I can but won't. But this time I just can't."

"You mean you don't know the answer?" asked Annie.

"I know part of the answer," replied Eulalie. "You've got to get out of the choice you made. After that, I don't know."

Annie snorted unhappily. "No one seems to know," she said.

"There is one thing I *do* know," said Eulalie.

Annie looked at her. "What's that?"

Eulalie pointed to the painting hanging on her wall. It was one Annie had done, and it depicted herself, Kate, and Cooper standing with their hands held up and joined together. Annie had given it to Eulalie as a gift. "I know that you're going to find the answer there," she said.

Annie looked at the image she'd painted. To her it represented the friendship and the magic that came together when she, Cooper, and Kate joined together in a circle. But how was that the answer to her problem? Cooper had already suggested forming their own coven, and they had decided against it. Besides, Kate and Cooper had chosen their covens already. Annie didn't see how they could help with her situation.

She looked back at Eulalie. "Thanks," she said.

"You just keep thinking about that picture," Eulalie said. "It will come to you."

"Maybe," said Annie. She stood up. "I have to get back home," she said. "But I'll come see you in a week or so, okay?"

Eulalie nodded. "I'll still be here," she said. She got a peculiar look on her face for a minute, and then she smiled broadly. "Oh, and Ben says he'll see you at your initiation."

Annie nodded. "Bye," she said, waving as she left the room.

As she walked back to her car, Annie pondered

her encounter with Eulalie. Just like the Caterpillar with Alice, the old woman had said some things that didn't make sense. Really she had just confirmed what Annie already knew—that she had to get out of joining the Daughters of the Cauldron. But apart from that, Eulalie hadn't really told her anything. And as far as Ben being with her at initiation, Annie wasn't sure she herself would even be there.

"Curiouser and curiouser," Annie said, repeating one of Alice's famous lines as she left Shady Hills and returned to her car. She really was starting to feel like Alice, lost in Wonderland, trying to navigate her way through a world that kept throwing new challenges at her and people who answered her questions with even more questions. She had accepted that she was going to have to tell Sophia she wasn't joining the Daughters of the Cauldron after all. But she didn't know what would happen after that. If there was no coven for her to join, would they just decide not to initiate her at all? That seemed the only likely response. But she couldn't worry about that, not yet.

First things first, Annie told herself as she turned the car away from the direction of home and drove toward the wharf area. It was time for her to talk to Sophia, and she wanted to do it face-to-face.

By the time she actually walked into Crones' Circle, she'd almost convinced herself not to do it. Even while driving around looking for a spot she'd been tempted to just go home, to simply call

Sophia. *Or maybe send her an e-mail*, she'd even thought at one point. She just couldn't stand the idea of facing her teacher, friend, and almost coven mate and telling her that she'd made a mistake.

Too late now, Annie thought sadly as she saw Sophia emerge from the back of the store.

"Hello there," Sophia said cheerfully. "To what do we owe this visit? I didn't expect to see you until next Thursday."

"I know," Annie said. "I just wanted to talk to you about something." She looked around the store. There were a couple of customers browsing around, and Robin, one of the store workers, was showing somebody the different candles they had for sale. "Could we go in back?" Annie asked Sophia.

"Sure," Sophia said. "Robin, can you watch the register for a minute?" she asked the other woman.

Robin nodded and Sophia led Annie to the back room.

"What's on your mind?" Sophia asked as soon as they were alone.

Annie tried to think of how to begin. *Not that it matters*, she told herself. *The ending will be the same no matter what you do.*

"I think I made a mistake," Annie said quickly, before she could change her mind. "I don't think I belong in the Daughters of the Cauldron."

Sophia's smile faded a little. "Oh," she said. "Can I ask why?"

Annie grimaced. "That's the embarrassing part,"

she said. "I don't really know why. It's just this feeling that I have. It's not that there's anything wrong with the coven. It's me." She paused and said it again. "It's me, not you."

Sophia laughed. "That's like a bad breakup line," she said.

Annie clapped her hand to her forehead. "That's exactly what I was afraid of," she said. "I'm sorry."

Sophia came over and put her arms around Annie. "It's okay," she said consolingly. "I'm just wondering what's making you feel this way."

"I wish I knew," Annie said. "I've been over and over it. I love all of you guys. I love the coven. But when it comes down to it, I just think I belong somewhere else."

"Where?" Sophia asked her.

Annie sighed again. "That's the rest of the problem," she said. "I don't know. I don't think any of the other covens are right for me either."

Sophia let go of Annie and stepped back, looking at her. "That *is* a problem," she said. "It's hard to initiate someone when there's no coven to initiate her into."

"Isn't there some kind of, I don't know, generic initiation?" Annie asked hopefully.

Sophia shook her head. "I'm afraid not," she said.

"I thought you might say that," replied Annie sadly.

"I have to say, you've taken me by surprise," Sophia told her. "However, I know you well enough to know that you don't act rashly. If you feel that the Daughters of the Cauldron isn't the coven for you, then I think that's the right decision."

"Except that it leaves me with no coven at all," said Annie.

Sophia looked at her for a moment. "Let me think about this," she said finally. "Maybe there's an answer somewhere."

"If there is, I hope you find it," said Annie, looking at Sophia and smiling weakly. "Because I sure can't."

CHAPTER 18

On Saturday, Kate and Cooper went over to Annie's house to help get things ready for the wedding the next day. When they arrived, Annie met them at the door.

"Quick," she said. "Get in here. We need reinforcements. Aunt Sarah has gone completely insane."

"What's she doing?" Cooper asked as Annie hustled them into the house.

"She's all freaked out," Annie answered. "Juliet says it happens to every bride the day before the wedding. Something about their being convinced that everything will go wrong."

At that moment Annie's aunt appeared. Her hair was disheveled and she was holding two different earrings up to her ears.

"Which ones?" she asked the girls, sounding a little hysterical.

"The small ones," Annie said quickly.

Cooper and Kate nodded. Aunt Sarah looked

relieved. "Thank you," she said, turning and disappearing up the stairs.

"It's been like this all morning," Annie said as she led her friends into the kitchen. "Grayson and Becka went to the grocery store to get away from it. Juliet is finishing the last-minute touches on the costumes. I'm stuck here making bags of birdseed for everyone to throw."

The kitchen table was spread with piles of netting, a bowl of birdseed, and several spools of different colored ribbon. The girls sat down and Annie showed them how to take one of the squares of netting, place birdseed in the center, and then tie it up with the ribbon so that it made a little bag.

"How many of these are we making?" asked Cooper as she picked up a piece of netting.

"Only about forty," Annie answered.

"Hey."

They all jumped as Aunt Sarah surprised them by popping into the kitchen. When they turned to look at her, she had a concerned expression on her face.

"Should we have ordered an ice swan?"

Kate and Cooper looked at Annie, who shook her head patiently. "No," she said. "Remember, we decided on a nice flower arrangement for the table."

"Oh," said Aunt Sarah. "Right." She scurried out of the kitchen, off on some other errand.

"Amazing," Cooper said, tying up her first bundle of birdseed. "People get so funny when they're under pressure. I hope we're not like that during our initiations."

Neither Kate nor Annie said anything. Cooper looked at them. "What?" she said. "Did I say something wrong?"

Annie cleared her throat. "I have something to tell you guys," she said. "I may not be getting initiated."

Kate and Cooper stopped working on their birdseed bags and just stared at Annie. Kate in particular seemed shocked.

"You're not getting initiated?" she asked.

"Maybe not," answered Annie.

"What happened?" Cooper inquired. "I thought you were all set to join the Daughters of the Cauldron."

"I was," Annie said. "But the more I thought about it, the more it just didn't feel right. So yesterday I went and told Sophia that I didn't think I should do it. If I can't find another coven I want to join, I probably won't be initiated."

To everyone's surprise, Kate laughed. She put her bag of birdseed on the table and sat there, shaking as she giggled more and more loudly.

"I don't think this is funny," said Cooper, giving Kate a displeased look.

"No," Kate said. "It's not funny. Only it sort of is, because this morning I called Thatcher and told him I didn't think I should be initiated by the Coven of the Green Wood."

Suddenly the attention turned to Kate. She wiped her eyes, which had started to tear, and looked at her friends. "I was trying to figure out how to tell you guys," she said. "It never occurred to me that Annie might beat me to it."

"And what's *your* excuse?" Cooper demanded.

"The same as Annie's," Kate said. "I thought I was really sure about joining the Coven of the Green Wood. But the more I thought about it, the more I realized that I was just doing it because it was the safe thing to do, not because I really thought it was the best place for me to be."

"What did Thatcher say?" Annie asked her.

"He understood," said Kate. "He was disappointed, but he understood. I still haven't told Sophia. Or Tyler," she added.

"I can't believe this," Cooper said, sitting back in her chair and looking at her friends in amazement. "Last week I was the one who wasn't being initiated and you two were all set. Now I'm the *only* one doing it?"

Kate and Annie looked at her and nodded.

"It looks that way," Kate said. "Unless we can find another coven, and I can't say any of the other ones appealed to me all that much."

"Same here," said Annie.

Cooper was dumbfounded. "Great," she said when she could finally speak. "Wonderful."

Annie put her hand on Cooper's arm. "It's not like Kate or I planned this," she said.

Cooper looked up at her. "If we'd started our own coven, this wouldn't be a problem," she said.

Annie shook her head. "That's not the answer either," she said. "Maybe if we had more experience, but not right now."

"So what, then?" asked Cooper, sounding exasperated. "You guys just don't do anything?"

"I still think there's an answer," Kate said. "I just don't know what it is."

"Well, time is running out," Cooper said. She groaned. "I don't believe this," she said again. "What else could go wrong?"

A scream pierced the air in answer. A moment later Annie's aunt tore into the kitchen, a look of utter horror on her face.

"What?" said Annie, leaping up.

"The minister," Aunt Sarah said. "I just got a phone call. She came down with the flu. Her daughter said she couldn't even come to the phone. She's not going to be able to make it."

"No minister?" Kate said. "You can't have a wedding without a minister."

"I know!" Aunt Sarah shrieked. "That's it. It's a sign. We have to call everything off."

"Calm down," Annie said soothingly, taking her aunt by the arm and putting her into one of the chairs. She turned to Kate. "Get her some tea, will you?"

As Kate went to get a cup and a tea bag from the cabinet, Annie talked to her aunt.

"We'll find you a minister," she told Aunt Sarah. "It can't be that hard. There are lots of ministers in town."

"Ones that will marry people dressed in *Alice in Wonderland* costumes?" her aunt said, clearly on the brink of losing it. "On such short notice?"

"I'm sure we can think of something," Annie said.

Kate brought Aunt Sarah her tea and handed it to her. Aunt Sarah took a sip, and indeed seemed to relax a little, although her hands were still shaking.

"Wait a minute," Cooper said suddenly, and everyone looked at her. "The person who marries you just has to be a licensed member of the clergy, right? It doesn't matter what religion."

Aunt Sarah shook her head. "I don't think it matters," she said. "Why?"

Cooper looked at her friends. "We know several licensed members of the clergy," she said, smiling.

Annie snapped her fingers. "Right," she said. "We do."

"Who?" asked Kate, a little slow to figure out what her friends were talking about.

"Thatcher, for one," Cooper said.

"And Sophia," added Annie. "Remember, they became licensed so they could do handfastings for coven members," she explained, referring to the Wiccan term for weddings.

"Do you think they would do this?" asked Kate.

"All we can do is ask," replied Annie. "Would

that be okay with you?" she asked her aunt.

Aunt Sarah nodded. "I'll be married by circus clowns as long as it's legal," she said.

"I'll call Sophia right now," said Annie.

She left the kitchen and returned a minute later holding the phone. "Sophia wants to know if she can come over to talk to you about the wedding," she told her aunt.

"Tell her to come right now if she can," said Aunt Sarah.

"Did you hear that?" Annie said into the phone. She laughed. "Okay, we'll see you then."

"What did she say?" asked Aunt Sarah as soon as Annie had hung up.

"She said she's hopping on her broom right away," Annie answered. "She'll be here in twenty minutes."

"Thank God," Aunt Sarah said, sounding completely relieved.

"No," Annie corrected her. "Thank *Goddess*."

Aunt Sarah got up. "I'm going to go lie down for a few minutes," she said. "Either that or throw up, I can't tell which. Call me when Sophia gets here."

She left the room, leaving the three girls to finish making the birdseed bags.

"She really said she would do it?" Cooper asked as they resumed work.

"She said she'd be happy to," Annie told her. "I guess she's forgiven me for dumping her."

Kate snorted. "Wait until she finds out I've

dropped out, too," she said.

"Makes me look pretty good, doesn't it?" Cooper said, grinning at them. "The one who was almost left back is now the class valedictorian."

"Just worry about your birdseed," Annie told her.

That's exactly what all of them did until there was a knock on the door a little while later. Annie went to answer it and came back with Sophia. Sophia eyed the bags of birdseed. "There will be some happy sparrows tomorrow afternoon," she said. "You guys have been busy."

"Yeah, well, you're the one who's saving the day," said Annie. "For a minute there I thought Aunt Sarah was a goner."

"I'll take care of her," Sophia said. "But first I want to talk to the three of you."

The girls looked at one another.

"Kate, Thatcher told me about your decision not to join the Coven of the Green Wood," Sophia said.

Kate blushed. "I was going to call you later today," she said.

"That's all right," said Sophia. "I called to see if he would help me officiate tomorrow. It just came up. Nobody is mad."

"Are you sure?" Kate asked doubtfully.

"I'm sure," said Sophia. "I'd rather have initiates be absolutely certain of their choices than have them choose just because they think they have to. Trust me, we've had people do that before and it turned out to be a disaster."

"I was afraid I was letting everyone down," Kate said.

"Well, I know Thatcher would love to have you in the coven," Sophia said. "Just as I would love to have Annie. But we respect your decisions. We may think you'd be right for our covens, but you're the ones who know for sure."

"It wasn't easy deciding not to do it," Kate said. "And I still haven't told Tyler."

Sophia smiled at her. "That conversation will probably be harder than the one you had with Thatcher," she said knowingly.

"So two of us are out," Annie said. "At least there's one of us left in the game."

"Not quite," Sophia said.

Cooper looked at her in disbelief. "No way," she said. "Don't tell me you've changed your minds about letting me be initiated? That is so not fair!"

Sophia held up her hands. "We haven't changed our minds," Sophia said.

"Then what is it?" demanded Cooper.

"It's the Children of the Goddess," Sophia replied.

"They don't want me?" said Cooper, stunned. "But Hunter said—"

"It's not that they don't want you," Sophia said, interrupting her. "It's just that they're having a few—organizational problems."

"What kind of problems?" Annie asked her.

Sophia paused, clearly thinking of the best way to tell them what was happening. "Oh, there's no other way to say this," she said, laughing a little. "Hunter and his girlfriend broke up. They were the ones who ran the coven, and at the moment things are a little chaotic. They're arguing over who's going to run it."

"I'm not getting initiated because the coven leaders *broke up*?" Cooper said, as if it was the stupidest thing she'd ever heard. "That would only happen to me."

"Actually, it happens more frequently than you might think," Sophia informed her. "Covens fall apart for all kinds of reasons."

"Well," Cooper said sarcastically. "It looks like all three of us are covenless. Maybe we should start a shelter for witches who need homes."

"This is weird," said Kate. "All three of us."

"Yeah," Annie said. "I thought I was going to be the only one."

"Me, too," said Kate.

"And I thought I was a sure thing," added Cooper.

Sophia was looking at the three of them. "There may be a solution," she said.

The girls looked at her eagerly.

"But I can't say anything right now," Sophia continued.

A collective groan rose from the table.

"What do you mean you can't tell us?" Cooper

said. "What kind of tease is that?"

"Just bear with me," said Sophia. "I'll know more tomorrow. We'll talk then. But in the meantime, don't assume it's over. Now I should go up and talk to Sarah. She's probably wondering where I am."

"You can't say something like that and then not tell us the rest!" exclaimed Annie.

"I'm sorry," Sophia replied. "I know it's an awful way to leave you. But I wanted you to know that there might be a chance this will all work out. I promise, I'll tell you everything tomorrow."

She left the girls in the kitchen and went upstairs to see Annie's aunt.

"What was that supposed to mean?" Kate asked when Sophia was gone. "How could things possibly work out?"

"Maybe we've been traded to another coven," suggested Cooper dryly. "For one head priestess and three initiates to be named later."

"All we can do is wait and see," said Annie, picking up a piece of netting and spooning some birdseed into it. "In the meantime, we have a wedding to get ready for."

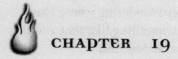

CHAPTER 19

"The house looks amazing," Kate told Annie as she carried boxes of food into the house on Sunday morning. She was helping her mother set up for the reception, and they had just arrived with the pastries, cakes, and sandwiches for what was going to be their version of a Mad Tea Party.

"We were up most of the night," Annie said, yawning. "Do you have any idea how many paper roses it takes to cover a stairway?"

The stairway was only one of the things that had been decorated. Annie, Juliet, Becka, and Meg had attached paper roses to practically everything. They'd sent Aunt Sarah and Grayson out for a relaxing dinner and gone to work, covering the house in pink, red, and white flowers so that it really would resemble a garden gone out of control. Mixed in with the paper roses were huge arrangements of real ones, brought early that morning by the florist. Juliet was running around putting them in just the right spots so that the scent would fill the whole house.

Kate took the boxes into the kitchen and put them on the counter. Her mother arrived a moment later, also carrying boxes.

"I never want to see another tart again," she said as she added her load to the one Kate had deposited on the counter. "Lemon tarts, peach tarts, strawberry tarts, blueberry tarts—I don't think there's one more thing I could possibly cram into a tart."

"They look delicious," commented Annie as she lifted the lid of one of the boxes and peered inside.

"Don't touch them!" Mrs. Morgan warned her. "Not until the reception."

Annie lowered the lid as Kate said jokingly, "Back away from the tarts."

Just then Jessica and Tara arrived with more boxes, this time containing sandwiches. Mrs. Morgan told them where to put everything and then turned to Kate and Annie. "Everyone out of the kitchen who isn't working," she said. "Now go. Shoo."

"We're going. We're going," said Kate as she and Annie fled into the other room, giving Tara and Jessica sympathetic glances.

"How is everything going?" Kate asked when she and Annie were alone.

"Fine," Annie said. "The food is here, the flowers are here. Juliet is upstairs doing last-minute costume stuff. Aunt Sarah and Grayson are only slightly hysterical. Becka and Meg are setting up the chairs in the garden. The string quartet called to say they'd be here at ten, and Sophia and Thatcher are due any minute."

"Speaking of which," Kate said, "any idea what Sophia is up to with this initiation thing?"

Annie shook her head. "None," she said. "I've been so busy, though, that I haven't even had time to think about it. How about you?"

"I have no clue," Kate said. "But I wish I did."

"Kate, I need your help bringing the cake in," Mrs. Morgan said, emerging from the kitchen holding her cell phone to her ear. "The delivery van is pulling up now. We'll bring the cake through the back door."

"You'd think she was directing the Oscars," said Kate, rolling her eyes. "I'll be back."

Kate left to help her mother, and Annie went upstairs to see how Juliet was doing. She found her making some adjustments to the Queen of Hearts costume that Sophia was going to wear. Because Sophia was a smaller size than the woman who had originally been performing the ceremony, Juliet had had to take it in. She was just sewing the final seam when Annie appeared.

"This feels like opening night at the theater," Juliet joked. "I'm waiting for someone to split their pants or rip something right before the curtain goes up."

"There's still time," Annie told her. "What did you decide about Thatcher's costume?"

Because they had planned on having only one

person perform the wedding, they hadn't thought about a possible second costume. But Sophia and Thatcher were going to do the wedding together, and they couldn't have one of them in costume and one of them in regular clothes.

"Ah," Juliet replied. "That one took some thought. "At first I thought he should be the King of Hearts, to go with the Queen. But I didn't have time to make that kind of costume."

"So what did you come up with?" Annie asked.

Juliet went to the table where she'd set up Aunt Sarah's sewing machine, and picked up a cloak made out of silver silk. There was a matching pair of silver pajamalike pants to go with it.

"The White Knight," she said. "I know this isn't exactly armor, but it will have to do. And Thatcher has that wild hair and beard. He'll make a great White Knight."

Annie laughed. "It's perfect," she said. "I can't wait to see the two of them all dressed up."

"Annie!" Becka called from downstairs.

"Duty calls," Annie said to Juliet, and left the room. When she got downstairs she found both Thatcher and Sophia and the string quartet waiting for her. She pointed at Sophia and Thatcher. "You two, upstairs," she said. Then she pointed at the quartet. "You four, come with me."

While Thatcher and Sophia went upstairs to get changed into their costumes, Annie showed the quartet into the garden, dodging Kate's mother and her helpers on the way through the kitchen.

"The wedding procession will come in through there," Annie said, indicating the back gate of the garden. "We'll walk between the rows of chairs and stop here," she continued, pointing to the spot they'd chosen for the actual wedding ceremony. "So you should probably set up over there," she concluded, waving her hand at a spot by the back steps.

"I hope the weather holds," said the woman who played the cello as the musicians began to set up. "It looks pretty gray."

Annie looked up at the sky. She'd been so busy preparing things that she hadn't even noticed the weather. But the cellist was right—it did look gray. She couldn't think about that, though. There was too much to do. Guests would be arriving in less than twenty minutes, and she wasn't even dressed.

Becka and Meg had finished setting up the forty or so chairs. Annie left the quartet to finish getting ready and herded her sister and Becka inside to get dressed. Everything seemed to be going smoothly, so she pushed her momentary worries about the weather to the back of her mind and concentrated on what came next.

The three girls went upstairs, where they found Thatcher and Sophia already costumed. Sophia looked gorgeous in the Queen of Hearts dress, and Thatcher was every inch the White Knight in his silver suit. His mane of gray hair was teased into a wild mess, and he was braiding his long beard with white ribbons.

"How are Grayson and Aunt Sarah?" Annie asked Juliet.

"They're fine," her sister answered. "You three go get dressed in your room. I'll take care of everyone else. Here are your costumes."

She piled the costumes into the girls' arms and sent them away. Annie, Becka, and Meg went to Annie's room, which now seemed to be the only part of the house not filled with people, and began dressing. Before long they were all outfitted, and Annie was helping Meg put on her rabbit nose, whiskers, and long white ears.

"You have too many arms," Meg remarked as one of Annie's dozen legs tickled her face.

"How do I look?" asked Becka, modeling her Cheshire Cat suit.

"Turn," Annie said, and Becka gave a slow twirl.

"Very nice," Annie said. "How about me?"

"Your head is a little crooked," Becka told her. "Here, I'll fix it."

She made some adjustments to the green hood Annie and Juliet had devised. It had two small antenna on top, which bobbled as Annie moved.

"Perfect," Becka said.

The three of them stood together and looked in the full-length mirror on the back of Annie's closet door. Meg twitched her nose. Becka meowed. Annie tried looking mysterious.

"I think we're ready," she said.

There was a knock on the door and Cooper came in.

"Hey," she said. "I was sent up to tell you that everything is just about ready. Juliet says you should all come down."

They all filed out of the room and down the stairs. Meg and Becka went first, followed by Annie and Cooper.

"You realize this is totally weird," Cooper said as they went down.

"Totally," Annie replied. "But so cool."

"*Very* cool," Cooper said, grinning. "So, did you get anything out of Sophia?" she asked.

"I haven't had time," answered Annie. "She said she'd tell us later. I guess we'll just have to wait."

Downstairs, Juliet had gathered everyone in the living room. Grayson and Aunt Sarah were still nowhere to be seen, and Annie figured Juliet was trying to keep them out of sight as long as possible.

"Okay," she said. "The guests are all in the garden. Thatcher and Sophia are there, too, and Grayson is standing with them. You three are going to go out the front door and go in through the back gate. Then Aunt Sarah will come in. After that, it's Thatcher and Sophia's show. Everybody ready?"

Annie, Meg, and Becka looked at one another.

"Ready," Annie said.

"Let's do it," Juliet said, beaming.

She led them outside and to the garden gate. The quartet was playing, and Annie saw all the guests sitting in their chairs, waiting for the wedding to start. Grayson, dressed in his Mad Hatter outfit, was standing with Thatcher and Sophia, looking very nervous.

"He's so cute," Becka said, looking at her father.

"I'm going to go get the bride," Juliet told them. "When the quartet starts playing the Mozart piece, you start walking. And here are your flowers."

She handed each of them a small bouquet of pink roses, then left them to go fetch Aunt Sarah.

"Meg, you'll go first," Annie told her sister. "Becka will be in the middle, and I'll go last. Ready?"

Before anyone could answer the quartet began playing Mozart. Annie opened the garden gate and Meg walked through. The guests, sensing that things were beginning, turned to look at her, oohing and aahing at her White Rabbit costume. They did the same when, a few seconds later, Becka followed Meg into the garden.

Annie, going last, looked at the faces of the invited guests as she walked down the aisle between the chairs. She couldn't believe that her aunt was actually about to get married. But there they were, walking toward Grayson as he smiled wildly.

Watching him, Annie wanted to laugh, but she kept her composure during her walk, stopping beside Becka and turning to face the garden gate.

The quartet began playing another piece, this one by Bach. Aunt Sarah had picked it, deciding against the traditional wedding march. Hearing it, everyone's eyes were on the gate as Aunt Sarah stepped through. Her Alice costume was perfect, right down to the blue bow in her hair, and Annie felt herself choking up as her aunt began her walk down the aisle, her bouquet of white roses trembling slightly.

She'd gotten halfway down the rows of chairs when the sound of thunder interrupted the quartet's playing. A moment later, raindrops began to fall. Annie looked up and saw ominous black clouds swirling overhead. *This is no little shower*, she thought. *This is a storm.*

She looked at her aunt, who had stopped walking, and then at Grayson, who was looking at the raindrops on his purple velvet coat as if he couldn't believe they were there. Several of the guests were holding purses over their heads in preparation for the downpour that threatened to begin any second.

No one said anything for a long, horrible moment. Then Annie heard Thatcher's booming voice call out, "Everyone into the house! Quickly!"

There was confusion as people stood up and dashed for the garden gate, swarming around Aunt Sarah as they headed for the front door and the safety of the house. Annie's aunt watched them going by her, as if she couldn't believe what was happening.

Annie felt Sophia take her arm. That broke the trance she was in, and she followed everyone else toward the house. Grayson had taken Aunt Sarah's hand, and the two of them were walking quickly out of the garden.

It's all ruined, Annie thought as she ran for the house. No sooner had she gotten inside than the rain came in earnest, falling in heavy sheets. Looking out the window, Annie watched it with a sense of sadness. She'd wanted her aunt's day to be perfect, and now everything had gone wrong.

Then she heard laughter. *Who could laugh at a time like this?* she thought angrily. She turned to see who was being so rude, and was surprised to see that the sound was coming from her aunt and from Grayson, who were holding on to each other and giggling madly.

"Oh, this is too funny," her aunt said when she could catch her breath.

Annie stared at her, wondering if her aunt had truly lost her mind. How could she think that having her wedding rained out was funny? But a moment later someone else joined in the laughter. It was Thatcher. His eyes sparkled as he chuckled along with the bride and groom.

"I told you that was a rain dance we did this morning, and not a good luck dance," he said to Sophia, pretending to be serious.

Several other people laughed at his remark. It seemed to lighten the mood, and even Annie found herself smiling.

"Come on," Thatcher called out. "There's no reason we can't do this wedding inside."

He led Sophia to the big staircase, where they stood a few steps up so that everyone could see them. Aunt Sarah and Grayson stood just below them, and Meg, Becka, and Annie lined up at the bottom. The guests gathered around, looking on, and Thatcher and Sophia began the service.

"We are gathered here in this lovely entrance-way to join together Sarah Crandall and Grayson Dunning," Thatcher said merrily. "They have asked you, their friends and family, to be with them as they share their vows."

"As you can see, this is hardly a traditional service," Sophia continued, making everyone laugh again. "So instead of the usual 'do you take this man and woman' stuff, the bride and groom have decided to say their own vows." She looked at Aunt Sarah and Grayson, who were standing there holding hands. "You're on," she said.

Aunt Sarah looked at Grayson. "I really do feel like Alice in Wonderland," she said. "I never expected to meet someone like you, or to be standing here like this. Sometimes I still think it's a dream. But even if it is, that's okay, because I've never been happier. I can't think of anyone I'd rather take this strange and wonderful trip with than you, and I promise that as long as we're on it I'll walk beside you and share whatever happens with you."

Grayson smiled. "I never thought this would happen to me, either," he said. "But from the first time I saw you, I knew something had changed. It felt like taking the first step on a new adventure. Every day since then, I've discovered new things to love about you, and about our life together. And I promise you that wherever this adventure takes us, we'll go there together. Even if it rains," he added, making the guests laugh.

"And now for the rings," Thatcher said. He reached into the pocket of his shirt and pulled out two rings. Annie watched as he handed one to Grayson and the other to her aunt.

"In ancient times, rings were symbolic of promises," Sophia said. "Kings gave rings to their knights when they sent them on quests. Queens gave rings to warriors who fought in their names. A ring given to someone else was a pledge, a physical reminder that a bond existed between two people. By placing these rings on each other's hands, you are symbolizing your promise to love one another, to share in life's challenges."

Grayson placed the ring he held on Aunt Sarah's finger. She did the same for him. Watching them exchange the simple bands of gold they'd picked out, Annie found herself filled with joy. In a way, she realized, her aunt and Grayson were undergoing their own initiation. They were beginning a life together, and the wedding ceremony was the ritual that marked that beginning.

"And now, by the power vested in me as the Queen of Hearts and the ruler of Wonderland, I pronounce you Alice and Hatter," Sophia said.

Everyone cheered as Grayson took Aunt Sarah in his arms and kissed her. The quartet, which had set up again in the living room, began to play.

"And now for tea!" Grayson called out, turning to face the guests.

Everybody began talking as Aunt Sarah and Grayson descended the steps and led the party into the dining room. There Mrs. Morgan had laid the table as if for a huge tea party. Mounds of tarts, cakes, pastries, and little sandwiches covered the table. In the center, the wedding cake sat. It was decorated with hundreds of wildflowers made out of sugar and icing, and it resembled some kind of wild bouquet picked from a garden gone out of control.

People began eating, and soon the wedding party was in full swing as people moved from room to room, talking and devouring the wonderful food. Kate's mother, helped by Tara and Jessica, made sure the plates were never empty, and everyone had a wonderful time.

"So, do you feel like an old married woman yet?" Annie asked her aunt when she could finally get close enough to her to talk to her.

"Not quite," her aunt said. "But this has certainly been the maddest tea party I've ever been at. Thank you for all your help."

"Any time," Annie said, giving her aunt a hug. "Not that there's going to be a next time or anything," she said. "I mean, this *will* be your last wedding."

Aunt Sarah laughed. "Yes," she said. "It will."

Annie left her to speak to other guests and joined Cooper and Kate, who were standing together munching on tarts and talking.

"Man, this could have been a disaster," she said.

"But it wasn't," Cooper told her. "In fact, this is the best wedding I've ever been at."

"Thatcher and Sophia were fantastic," agreed Kate.

"Speaking of Sophia, I think it's time we cornered her," Annie said. "Where is she?"

"Over there," Cooper said, nodding in Sophia's direction. "Shall we?"

"Let's," said Kate, and the three of them walked over to their teacher, who was eating a raspberry tart.

"I wondered how long you'd be able to stand it," Sophia said as the girls looked at her expectantly.

"So what's this big announcement?" Cooper asked.

"Yeah," Kate said. "Spill it. We can't stand the suspense anymore."

Sophia finished the last bit of tart and licked her fingers. "Well," she said, "I was thinking about this whole initiation situation. I've been doing this long enough to know that having three people left without covens right before initiations means *something* is going on—especially three people like you. I knew this wasn't just coincidence."

The three friends looked at one another. What was Sophia getting at?

"I did a little ritual about it," Sophia continued. "You know, had a few words with the lady up there," she said, looking up toward the sky.

"And what did she have to say about it?" Annie asked impatiently.

"She told me the answer was right in front of my nose," Sophia said. "Which didn't really help until I talked to some of my coven mates about it. That's when it became clear."

"What did?" Cooper asked her. "Because it's not clear to me."

"A new coven," Sophia said.

"New coven?" Kate repeated.

Sophia nodded. "When I mentioned your problem to the coven, Archer told me that she's been thinking about forming a new coven."

"You mean leaving the Daughters of the Cauldron?" Annie said.

"Can she do that?" Kate asked.

Sophia nodded. "It's very common," she said. "Archer has been training with me for many years. While she likes the focus of the coven, she's reached a point where she thinks she would like to start a coven of her own, one where she can try out some new ideas. Several of the other members are also interested in being in it, as well as some people Archer knows from other activities." She looked at the three of them. "She'd like the three of you to join it as well."

Kate, Cooper, and Annie looked at each other in surprise and delight.

"A new coven," Annie said. "That would be exciting."

"I think it's a wonderful idea," Sophia told them. "Archer is a great teacher, and the three of you know her well. This would be a great opportunity for all of you." She paused. "What do you all think?"

The girls looked at one another for the briefest of pauses.

"Yes!" they all said in unison.

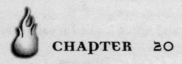

CHAPTER 20

Cooper sat across the table from Amanda Barclay, concentrating on wrapping her pasta around her fork so that she wouldn't have to say anything.

"How's your dinner, honey?" asked Mr. Rivers.

"Great," Cooper and Amanda said at the same time. They looked at one another for a moment, and then Amanda looked away, wiping her mouth on her napkin.

He calls her honey? Cooper thought. *I think I'm going to be sick.*

It was Monday, the day after the wedding. Cooper's father had called her that afternoon and asked her to have dinner with him and Amanda that evening. Cooper hadn't expected him to collect on her promise to him so soon, but a deal was a deal, and she'd had to accept the invitation. Now the three of them were sitting in an Italian restaurant, eating and attempting to make conversation.

"I spoke with Jane's parents yesterday," Mr. Rivers said.

That got Cooper's attention. Jane had called her the previous night to say that her father had spoken with Mr. Rivers, but Jane hadn't known any of the details. Cooper had been anxious to find out what had transpired. Her own mother had already agreed— if slightly reluctantly—to let Cooper play the tour.

"What did they say?" she asked her father, praying that it was good news.

"They have some of the same reservations your mother and I have," Mr. Rivers told her.

Here comes the no, Cooper thought, preparing herself for bad news. *But at least then your deal will be off and you won't have to have any more dinners with Newspaper Girl.* She glanced at Amanda, and saw with some measure of satisfaction that her enemy had gotten marinara sauce on her white blouse.

"I also spoke with Serena Mao," Cooper's father continued. "And she sounds like a trustworthy person. She assures me that she'll personally see to it that you and Jane don't get into any trouble on the road."

"So we can go?" Cooper asked, wanting to believe it was happening but afraid to in case her father was leading up to a letdown.

"You can go," Mr. Rivers said, smiling.

Cooper was so happy she almost knocked her water glass over as she jumped up to hug her father.

"Thank you!" she said. "You are the *best.*"

"That's why I'm your manager," her father told her.

Cooper sat down again. She still couldn't believe it had all been finalized. Even after her father had agreed that she could do it, she'd been convinced that *something* would happen to ruin it—like Jane's parents would say no, or Betty Bangs would change her mind. But now it all seemed to be falling into place.

This is going to be the most amazing summer of my life, she thought excitedly. She couldn't wait to get home and call Jane so they could start making plans. *Oh, and we'll have to write some new songs*, she told herself, her mind suddenly filling with all sorts of things that needed to be done.

"You haven't heard the best part," Mr. Rivers said.

Cooper looked at him. "There's more?" she said. What else could there possibly be? Her dream had just come true.

Mr. Rivers looked at Amanda. "Do you want to tell her?" he asked.

Amanda nodded and turned to Cooper.

If she tells me they're getting married, I'm going to die right here, thought Cooper, her heart pounding. What other kind of news began with a statement like the one her father had made?

"I spoke to an editor friend of mine today," Amanda told Cooper.

They're not getting married, thought Cooper with relief. She didn't care what else Amanda had to say as long as it didn't involve wedding plans—at least not wedding plans with Cooper's father.

"He works at *Rolling Stone*," Amanda continued.

"Uh-huh," said Cooper, turning back to her food and ignoring Amanda.

"He'd like me to do a story on the Bitter Pills," continued Amanda. "They want a feature article on up-and-coming bands featuring young women. I pitched him you and Jane, and he loved it. I'm going to follow you guys on the road for a while and write about your experiences."

Cooper stopped eating and stared at Amanda. "You're going with us on the road?" she said, dumbfounded.

Amanda nodded. "For a week," she said. "I'll write about you and some of the other bands."

She's going on the road with us, Cooper thought miserably. *Amanda is going to follow us*. Then another part of her brain kicked in and she thought, *For* Rolling Stone. *We're going to be in* Rolling Stone.

"We're going to be in *Rolling Stone*?" she asked Amanda, sure she'd somehow misheard her.

"Five thousand words," Amanda said. "And pictures."

Cooper looked from Amanda to her father and back again. She was overwhelmed with mixed emotions. Was this the same Amanda Barclay who had caused so much trouble for her the year before?

"I thought it might help make up for what happened last year," Amanda said, smiling shyly.

Cooper looked at her. Had she been wrong about

Amanda? Was there perhaps more to her than Cooper had seen? *If Dad likes her, there must be*, she thought. *Maybe you need to give her a chance. You know, kind of like Annie and Kate gave you a chance. Look how that turned out.*

Cooper returned Amanda's smile. "It's a good start, anyway," she said.

An hour later, Cooper was back home. The rest of dinner with Amanda and her father had been okay. They had talked some more about the tour, and Cooper had discovered that—as her father had tried to tell her—she and Amanda did have a few things in common. It turned out that Amanda was very familiar with Scrapple's music, and had once interviewed Betty Bangs for a newspaper piece. She'd always wanted to write about music, and the piece she was doing about the Bitter Pills would be her first big assignment for a magazine. She was excited about it, and talking to her made Cooper even more excited about the possibilities for the summer.

Less exciting was the prospect of telling her mother about her father's involvement with Amanda Barclay. Cooper knew the time had come for her to bring it up. If Amanda was going to be writing about her and Jane, Cooper thought it was only fair that her mother know how the connection had been made. So when she came downstairs and found her mother sitting in the living room and reading, she decided it was time for them to talk.

"How was dinner?" her mother asked, closing her book and setting it on the coffee table.

"Good," Cooper said. "Actually, it was great."

"How's your father?" Mrs. Rivers asked her.

"He's fine," said Cooper. "He worked things out with the Goldsteins and Serena Mao, and everything is on for the tour."

Her mother nodded. Cooper took a deep breath, wondering how she was going to bring up the issue of Amanda. Her mother had been through so much with the divorce and what came after that Cooper didn't want to do anything that might make her depressed or unhappy. But she had to say something.

"And how was Amanda?" asked her mother.

Cooper's mouth hung open in surprise. She looked at her mother, who had a slight smile on her face.

"How did I know?" Mrs. Rivers asked.

Cooper couldn't speak. She was so shocked to hear her mother say Amanda's name that she didn't know what to say. "Yeah," was all she could manage.

"Your father told me," her mother explained. "Well, he didn't exactly tell me on his own. I saw them out together one night when Mary and I went out to dinner. He and Amanda came into the same restaurant. So I asked him."

"You did?" Cooper said, amazed.

"Oh, not in front of her or anything," Mrs. Rivers said, laughing. "I waited until the next day. I'm afraid I wasn't as nice as I might have been about it."

"You and me both," Cooper said, thinking of her reaction to seeing her father with Amanda. She hesitated. "How are you about it now?"

Mrs. Rivers shrugged. "It's not the easiest thing in the world," she said. "But I've lived through worse. Besides, if he wants to go out with some skinny ditz with a bad dye job, who am I to complain?"

Cooper suppressed a laugh. She was making a conscious effort not to think terrible things about Amanda. But she couldn't resist giving her mother a conspiratorial grin. "I see you're handling it well."

"I can think of worse ways," her mother replied. "Besides, I've gotten better. You should have heard what I said to Mary about her."

Cooper rolled her eyes. "I can only imagine," she said, having heard T.J.'s mother dissect more than one person with her sharp tongue.

"I don't want you being mean to her, though," said Mrs. Rivers. "If your father likes her, that's what matters. Besides, maybe it's just a phase."

"Maybe," Cooper said. She would tell her mother about Amanda's *Rolling Stone* article later. For now she was just glad she didn't have to keep her father's relationship a secret.

"I'm going to go upstairs," Cooper said, standing up. "I have to talk to Annie and Kate about some initiation stuff."

"Actually, I wanted to talk to you about that," said her mother.

Cooper looked at her questioningly. "What

about it?" she asked. "You're okay with it, right?"

Mrs. Rivers nodded. "Yes," she said. "But I'm afraid I haven't been entirely honest with you about something."

Cooper sat down again, looking at her mother. What was she talking about?

Mrs. Rivers cleared her throat. "Your grandmother *was* a witch," she began. "I know I've told you that I wasn't really sure where she learned what she knew, but I do know. She learned it from her mother, who I'm sure learned it from her mother before her. Yes, a lot of what she knew was just basic Scottish folk magic. But there was more to it than that."

Cooper was fascinated. All this time she'd thought that what her grandmother practiced was simply small rituals and customs she'd learned growing up. But apparently there was more that she didn't know.

Mrs. Rivers got up and went to the desk that sat against one wall of the living room. She opened a drawer and took some things out. Coming back to the couch, she sat down and held the items in her lap. Cooper could see that one of them appeared to be a book of sorts. Her mother kept the other clasped in her hand, and Cooper couldn't see it.

"This was your grandmother's," she said, handing the book to Cooper. It was a small leather-bound volume. There was no title on the soft, worn cover, but when Cooper opened it she found page after page covered in fine, neat handwriting.

"It's her journal," Cooper said after reading a little bit of one page. She looked up at her mother. "She's written all kinds of things in here—spells she did, incantations—all sorts of things."

"I know," Mrs. Rivers told her daughter. "I found it in her things after she died."

"This is her Book of Shadows!" said Cooper, realizing what she held in her hands.

"I thought you might like to have it," her mother told her. "I remember her mother having one, too, but I don't know what ever happened to it. Probably it's been lost. But I'm sure a lot of what's in Mother's journal was copied from her mother's."

"This is fantastic," Cooper said, running her fingers over the pages. "Why did you keep it if you were so against the idea of being a witch?" she asked her mother.

Mrs. Rivers shrugged. "I'm not sure," she said. "There were many times when I was going to throw it out. Once I even started to burn it. But something stopped me every time, a feeling, like there was a reason to save it. Now I guess I know what that reason was."

Cooper was almost crying. She knew what it must mean to her mother to give her the Book of Shadows. It meant that she accepted Cooper as a witch. Even if she herself didn't really understand the draw of magic, she was embracing her daughter's decision to follow her grandmother into the Craft.

"There's something else," Mrs. Rivers said. She

opened her hand and Cooper saw something resting in her palm. It was a necklace, a talisman of some sort on a black cord.

"What is that?" asked Cooper, taking the necklace from her mother and holding it up for closer inspection.

"Your grandmother did have a group she practiced magic with," Mrs. Rivers said. "Every week she and some of her friends would gather at our house. I don't know what they did, really. I tried to stay away from it. I suppose they were—"

She couldn't finish the sentence, so Cooper did. "A coven," she said. "Grandma was in a coven."

"Yes," her mother said. "I suppose she was. Anyway, they all wore this talisman. One of the women made jewelry, and she created it."

Cooper looked at the talisman. It was circular. All around the circle ran an intricate line of knotwork. It had one central cross-shaped image surrounded by eight smaller knots. The design was unbroken, twisting and turning around on itself to form the image.

"It represents the Wheel of the Year," said Cooper, who had seen a similar design in a book. "Each of the smaller knots is one of the sabbats. The cross is one of the oldest Celtic images."

"Your grandmother always wore that," Mrs. Rivers told her. "She gave it to me right before she died. I think that's the first time I saw her without it. I remember when some of her friends who were still alive came to the funeral, they were all wearing them."

"It was her coven symbol," Cooper said, closing her fingers over the talisman. Having her grandmother's Book of Shadows was remarkable enough, but having the necklace almost meant more to her. She reached up and felt the pentacle that she wore around her own neck. It had caused her a lot of trouble, but it also made her feel very powerful, and very much a part of the Craft. It was a symbol of her commitment to Wicca, and wearing it was a constant reminder of how far she had come. She knew that the talisman she held must have been very important to her grandmother.

"I'll wear it at initiation," she told her mother.

Her mother nodded. "Your grandmother would be proud of you," she said. She looked at her daughter for a long moment. "And I'm proud of you, too."

Cooper gave her mother a hug. "Thank you," she said. "For everything."

When she pulled away from her mother, both of their eyes were wet with tears. "I wish she could see you now," Mrs. Rivers said.

"She can," Cooper said. "I'm sure she can."

CHAPTER 21

Annie handed Eulalie the flowers she'd brought with her. They were roses from the wedding, a dozen of the nicest ones arranged in a pretty vase. Eulalie took them and inhaled the scent, a smile spreading across her wrinkled face.

"Reminds me of home," she said. "Was it a good wedding?"

"The best," Annie told her.

Eulalie nodded. "You'll have to tell me all about it."

"Next time," said Annie. "I have to get back to the house. We're taking Juliet, Becka, and Grayson to the airport. But I wanted to stop by and tell you that you were right about my initiation."

"You don't say," Eulalie remarked, looking extremely satisfied with herself. "How so?"

Annie nodded at the painting on the wall. "We're all staying together," she said. "The three of us. It was just like you said—we had to remember the things that had brought us together in the first place."

"Mmm-hmm," Eulalie said, nodding. "The three of you belong together. I haven't even met these friends of yours, but I know that much."

"I'll bring them by to see you when I come next week," Annie told her. She bent down and kissed Eulalie's soft cheek. "But now I have to go."

"When's your initiation?" Eulalie asked as Annie turned to leave.

"Thursday," answered Annie.

Eulalie nodded again. "We'll be thinking about you," she said.

Annie smiled. "Tell Ben hello," she said as she left the room.

Back at her house, she helped load Juliet's bags into one car and Becka's and Grayson's bags into Grayson's rental car. Aunt Sarah and Meg rode with Grayson, while Juliet, Becka, and Annie took the other car. Annie got to drive, which made her feel very grown-up, even though she knew her aunt was watching her like a hawk from Grayson's vehicle.

"This week was so much fun," said Juliet as they traveled down the highway to the airport. "I can't wait to see the pictures."

"Your costumes made the wedding," said Annie. "Everyone loved them."

"I know I love mine," Becka said from the backseat. "I'm going to wear the ears to school tomorrow."

"Speaking of school, I can't wait for it to be over," Annie commented. "Then you guys can move here for good."

"Is that going to be weird?" Juliet asked Becka. "Leaving San Francisco, I mean?"

Becka shook her head. "There are things I'll miss," she said. "But this already feels like home."

Annie caught Becka's eye in the rearview mirror. She was thrilled that the two of them would be living in the same house soon. It already felt like they were sisters.

"And you've already got friends here," Annie said, thinking of Kate, Cooper, Sasha, Jane, and the assorted people they hung out with.

"And the class," Becka said.

"Class?" Juliet said. "What class?"

"Becka is joining the dedication class at Crones' Circle," Annie explained. "It starts up again right after she moves here."

Juliet shook her head and laughed. "Am I going to be the only person in this family who isn't a witch?" she said.

"Well, there's Meg," said Annie.

"So far," remarked Becka. "I heard her asking Sophia what a coven was at the reception."

"Goddess help us if she gets any ideas," said Annie.

"This is going to be a busy summer," Becka commented. "Class, going to see Cooper and Jane play, hanging out. I can't wait."

"And of course you'll have to make at least one trip to New Orleans," Juliet said. "You haven't lived until you've experienced one of our summers."

"My birthday is in August," said Becka. "Maybe I can convince Dad to let me come then."

"Perfect," said Juliet. "Just in time for the heat wave."

They arrived at the airport and parked the car. Grayson pulled in beside them and everyone piled out. After pulling the bags from the trunks, they walked inside and located the departure gates they needed by looking at the monitors located near the ticket counters.

"We're only a few gates apart," said Juliet.

"Great," Grayson replied. "We can all wait together."

After checking their luggage and getting their boarding passes, they made their way through the security area to the gates. A kind of awkward silence descended as they stood in a little group, waiting for the two flights to be called. For Annie, it was a moment that was both sad and happy. She was sorry to see Juliet, Grayson, and Becka go, but she kept reminding herself that she would see them all again soon.

"It seems strange marrying you one day and sending you off on a plane the next," Annie's aunt said to Grayson, making him laugh.

"This way you get some time to adjust to the idea of having a husband," he told her.

"Husband," said Aunt Sarah. "It sounds so odd saying the word now—my husband." She gave a bemused look.

"Does that mean I can call you Uncle Grayson?" Meg asked.

It was Grayson's turn to look amused. "How about you just call me Grayson?" he suggested. "Uncle makes me feel a little old."

"Hey!" Aunt Sarah said. "What does that make me?"

"Uh-oh," Grayson said. "Is this our first fight?"

Aunt Sarah eyed him. "If it is, who won?"

"Flight 1762 departing for San Francisco is now boarding at Gate B12," came the announcement over the loudspeaker.

"That's us," Grayson said. "Everyone say goodbye." He gave hugs to Meg, Juliet, and Annie. He gave a particularly long hug and kiss to Aunt Sarah. "I'll call you tonight," he said. "I love you."

"I love you, too," Aunt Sarah told him.

Becka hugged Meg, Aunt Sarah, and Juliet. Then she hugged Annie, clasping her tightly. "It's only a few more months," she said. "Then the real fun starts. Good luck at your initiation, and call me *immediately* afterward. I want all the details."

"I will," Annie said. "Say hello to the house for me."

The two girls separated, and Grayson and Becka walked to their gate. Annie and the others watched as they disappeared into the tunnel leading to the plane.

"I'm next," Juliet said.

They walked to her departure gate, where

people were lining up. The flight wouldn't board for a few minutes, so the four of them had a little more time to talk.

"It was so nice having you here," Aunt Sarah told her. "I still can't quite believe the baby I held all those years ago is standing in front of me."

"Well, it's all thanks to Annie," Juliet told her. She put her arm around her sister. "If she hadn't written to me, I never would have known all of you even existed. But now that I do, I'm looking forward to getting to know all of you better."

"Next time there's a trip to New Orleans, *I* want to go," Meg said forcefully.

"I think we can manage that," Aunt Sarah told her.

The boarding for Juliet's flight began, and she gave final hugs to Aunt Sarah and Meg. Then she took Annie's hands. "Good-bye, little sister," she said.

"Good-bye, big sister," replied Annie.

They embraced. "You made a good Caterpillar," Juliet whispered to her. "I bet you'll make an even better witch."

"I should have had you make me a costume," said Annie, her voice shaking.

"Tell you what, I'll send you one," Juliet joked as they let go, each of them wiping her eyes. "Will basic black be okay?"

Annie laughed. "Get on your plane," she said. "I'll send you those wedding pictures as soon as we get them."

Juliet waved one more time as she walked

through the gateway, and Annie was alone with her aunt and sister. They waited a moment and then began the walk back to the car.

"The house is going to seem so quiet," remarked Aunt Sarah. "I've gotten used to there being people everywhere."

"I can always invite a bunch of my friends over for a slumber party if you want," suggested Meg.

"Maybe later," said Aunt Sarah. "I could use a few days off. Getting married is *exhausting*."

They left the terminal and got into Aunt Sarah's car, having dropped the rental car keys off at the counter inside the airport. Driving home, Annie listened as her sister and her aunt talked. Her own thoughts were focused on Thursday, and the upcoming initiation ceremony. She, Cooper, and Kate had all talked with Archer on Sunday evening after the wedding festivities. Archer had explained more about the coven she wanted to start, telling them that it was going to be similar to the Daughters of the Cauldron but with more emphasis on teaching young witches and preparing them for leadership roles in covens of their own someday. She was forming it with a friend of hers who was currently part of another coven as well, and the two of them would be the main leaders, while the other members would all help to design rituals and run circles. The members were primarily going to be witches who had been practicing for only a few years, so that they would all learn together. Archer's hope was that they would create a new and vibrant coven that would grow into something different. The new faces of the old religion, she had called it, and Annie liked the description. It combined something ancient with something fresh and modern, and she was sure it was a place where she would feel right at home.

Now that she knew she was going to be joining a coven where she really felt she belonged, she was able to think more about exactly what might happen at the initiation. Because it was a new coven, Archer said, they would be both initiating new witches and doing a kind of initiation for the coven as a whole. She hadn't given them any details, but Annie was sure it was going to be something she would never forget.

"Since it's only eleven, I'm going to drop you guys off at school," Aunt Sarah said. "That way you can have the rest of the day there."

"Gee, thanks," said Meg sarcastically. "Like I really wanted *that*."

Aunt Sarah ignored her, humming happily to herself. Annie could see that already there was a change taking place in her aunt, a change for the better. *She's in love*, Annie thought happily as Aunt Sarah pulled up in front of Beecher Falls High School. Meg's school was farther down the road, so she would be dropped off second.

"See you later," Annie said as she got out of the car.

When she went inside, fourth period was just

ending. Students were pouring from the class-rooms, filling the halls with their conversations and the sounds of lockers opening and closing. For Annie, fifth period was a library period, so she didn't have to hurry. She knew her friends would all be heading to their various classes, and she would see them later at lunch. She'd brought her backpack with her, and the books and notebooks she needed were in it, making a trip to her locker unnecessary. For the moment all she had to do was walk leisurely to the library.

When she got there she pushed the doors open and went inside. A few other students were there, studying or talking quietly with friends as they pre-tended to work. Annie saw an empty table in the back and headed for it. She'd done most of her homework already, but she had some chemistry problems she'd saved to do later, and she thought she'd pass the period working on those. Chem was one of her favorite subjects, and she found working out the problems relaxing.

She sat down, took out her books, and began working on the first problem. She became engrossed in it almost immediately, and soon she blocked out everything but the formulas she scrib-bled in her notebook. But then she had the strange feeling that someone was watching her, and she looked up.

Sitting a few tables away from her was Brian Stoors. He was the guy Annie had dated for a while—until she'd written an editorial for the school paper about being into Wicca and he'd dropped her suddenly. Brian was sitting with some of his friends. He was looking at Annie and saying something to them. Annie saw one of the boys laugh.

The way Brian had broken up with her had always bothered Annie. He'd seemed like such a nice guy. They'd had some wonderful times, and he'd treated her well. At least until the editorial. Ever since then, he'd barely said two words to her.

Brian said something else, and the whole table laughed and looked at Annie. What was Brian saying? Annie had a feeling that whatever it was, it wasn't flattering.

She looked at the people Brian was hanging with. He was older than she was, a senior. All of his friends were seniors as well. Normally, Annie would have been afraid of guys like that, intimidated by them because they were older, bigger, and louder.

Now, though, she was just angry. How dare they make fun of her? How dare Brian say anything about her that would make people laugh at her? *Who does he think he is?* she thought angrily.

At the time she'd met Brian, Annie had been under the influence of the goddess Freya. Freya's presence had made her bolder than she would normally be, and she had flirted with Brian until he'd asked her out. Part of Annie was embarrassed about that. But another part of her remembered how good it had felt to be so in control, so confident. She wished she could be that way now. She wished she could tell Brian just what she thought about the way he'd treated her because of her interest in the Craft.

Wait a minute, she thought. *You are confident. Haven't you learned anything this year?*

She thought about that. She was about to be initiated as a witch. She *was* a strong, powerful, young woman. She wasn't the shy little Annie who had hidden behind her glasses and her good grades before meeting Kate and Cooper. She wasn't the timid Annie who had worried about not being liked by the popular kids. She was a different Annie, a girl who stood up for herself—and for Wicca.

It's time to graduate, she told herself.

Standing up, she shut her chemistry book, picked up her backpack, and strode over to the table where Brian and his friends were sitting.

"Is something funny?" she asked, standing in front of them with her hands on her hips.

Brian looked up and gave her a goofy smile. "No," he said. "Why?"

"Because it seems to me that you and your little buddies here are laughing at me," Annie said. "So I just thought I'd stop by to see if maybe you would let me in on the joke."

Brian's expression changed. He seemed less confident than he had a moment before. "No," he said. "Everything's fine."

"Ooh," one of his friends said. "Brian's afraid of the little witch."

"Yeah," said another. "What's the matter, you afraid Sabrina here is going to turn you into a toad?"

The guys laughed. Brian turned red.

"Nice friends you have," Annie told him. "I thought you were a better person than that." Then she looked at the guys seated around the table. "As for you morons, here's a clue—ten years from now, when you're all sitting around thinking about how high school was the best time of your lives, me and my friends will be the ones laughing at you. Because it's people like you who have to cling to their memories of their touchdowns and their cheerleader girlfriends and their prom dates when real life catches up with them and they figure out that all along they were the ones who were the real losers."

She turned and walked away, leaving the group of guys staring at her retreating back. None of them said a word, and as Annie walked toward the library doors and threw them open, she started laughing. She ran down the hall, laughing harder and harder, and at the end of it she pumped her fist in the air.

"Girl, you have *arrived!*" she told herself.

CHAPTER 22

"This was an interesting choice for a meeting place," Tyler said as he climbed onto the enormous rock and sat down beside Kate.

Kate looked out over the ocean. It was twilight, and the sea was painted purple, red, and gold as the sun melted into the horizon and the world moved from day to night. She loved this particular time of the day. Everything seemed bathed in magic. And sitting on the big rock that lay half on the beach and half in the water, she felt as if she were someplace truly special.

"I like it here," she told Tyler. "A lot of important things in my life have happened on this rock."

She thought about all of those things. She'd broken up with Scott there. She'd first kissed Tyler there. And just beyond the rock was the cove where she, Cooper, and Annie had done their first real ritual. It seemed that all of the paths she followed led back there, to the place where the sea met the earth. *Like a drop of rain*, she sang to herself, *flowing to the ocean*. She *was* that drop of rain, returning again and again to the ocean, to the Goddess.

"I guess you heard that I'm not joining the coven," Kate said, turning her head to look at Tyler.

"Thatcher mentioned it," he said simply. Kate could tell he was upset but didn't want to say anything.

"It just wouldn't work," Kate told him.

"What wouldn't?" asked Tyler.

Kate smiled to herself. She knew that Tyler was really asking if she meant her being in the coven or her being with him.

"Neither," said Kate. "The coven *nor* us."

Tyler nodded. "I figured you were going to say that," he replied darkly.

Kate was silent for a minute, watching the gulls swoop and dip over the waves, catching the tiny fish that rose to the surface to feed. Watching the big, noisy birds eat the fish in great, greedy mouthfuls had bothered her when she was a little girl. She'd resented them for what she saw as their picking on the smaller creatures. Now she saw it differently. *It's all part of the cycle*, she thought. *Everything dies and is reborn.* Her relationship with Tyler was sort of like that, she realized. She'd met him as her relationship with Scott was dying. Then, being with Tyler, she'd felt alive. But that relationship, too, had died. Maybe now, she thought, was the time for it to be born again in a new form.

"You know, when I met you I thought you were the answer to everything," she said to Tyler. Then she laughed.

"What?" Tyler said, hurt.

Kate put her hand on his arm. "I'm not laughing at you," she said kindly. "I'm laughing at me. I can't believe I ever let myself believe that someone—anyone—could make my life perfect."

"No one can make your life perfect," Tyler remarked. "But people can make your life better."

Kate nodded. "And you do," she said. "You *do*."

"Then can I ask why—once again—you've decided that you can't go out with me?" Tyler asked her.

Kate sighed deeply. "Part of it is the Annie thing," she said.

"I thought we were beyond that," Tyler said, pulling away from her hand.

Kate shrugged. "I am over it intellectually," she said. "I know neither of you meant to do anything hurtful. But sometimes understanding something in your head doesn't do anything to change how you feel in your heart."

"In other words, you're still angry."

"No," Kate said. "Not anymore. But something broke when you did what you did, something that tied me to you. And that can't be repaired."

"And that's why you decided not to be in the coven," said Tyler.

"Actually, no," Kate answered. "It's a part of the

reason, but a really small part. I admit that the idea of getting back together with you made me feel a little safer. It was like a familiar face in a roomful of strangers. Part of me thought that having what we used to have would make it easier for me to feel like I was home in the coven." She paused, putting her thoughts into words. "But sometimes you need to leave home," she continued. "Sometimes you need to look for something that will test who you are and what you can do."

"Meaning a new coven," Tyler said.

"Yeah," replied Kate. "What Archer is starting is exciting. It's a chance for me to be part of creating something new instead of trying to fit into something that already exists. I think I need that."

"Plus you get to stay with Annie and Cooper," said Tyler.

"I think we're meant to be together," Kate said dreamily. She was watching the clouds darken as night fell. "We came together because of magic, and I don't think that magic is finished yet. We still have work to do together."

Tyler took a deep breath and let it out. "Well, I'm going to miss you," he said.

Kate reached out and took his hand, holding it in hers. "No," she said. "You won't miss me, because now you can really get to know me. I don't think you and I ever really did that. Besides, I'm a different person now, not the one you met at that Ostara ritual."

"That I'll agree with," Tyler said.

"Friends?" Kate asked him.

"Friends," Tyler said. "Just promise me one thing?"

"What's that?" asked Kate.

"Don't become *too* many different people," said Tyler. "I don't think I can keep up."

They sat on the rock for a while longer, until it was dark and it had become a little too cold to sit in the wind any longer. Then they walked along the beach, talking, and climbed the stairs to the wharf.

"I've got to get home," Kate said. "Tomorrow's the big night, and I have some stuff I want to do to get ready."

Tyler nodded. "I guess I'll see you at the party afterward, then," he said.

Kate nodded. She hesitated a moment and then gave Tyler a hug. He held her, his arms around her back, and then let her go.

"Bye," he said, smiling and looking a little sad.

"Bye," Kate answered.

She turned and walked to the bus stop. She wondered how her relationship with Tyler would change in the coming weeks and months. Would they really become closer? She hoped so. He was a wonderful guy, and there was a lot about him she loved. But he wasn't the guy for her. Someday she would find that guy. *But I'm not in any hurry*, she told herself.

She rode the bus home and let herself into the

house. Her mother was still out, catering a party, and her father hadn't gotten home from the sporting goods store yet. Kate went into the kitchen, looked in the refrigerator to see what her mother had left for dinner, and took out a couple of containers. She was opening them, investigating the contents, when she had a sudden thought.

This is how it all started, she reminded herself. The day she'd brought the spell book home from the library, her parents had both been out. She'd had the house to herself, and she'd gone to her room and performed her first spell. Now, a year later, she was alone again on the night before her initiation. That gave her an idea.

She put the containers of food away and went upstairs to her room. Going to her closet, she removed the bag of ritual items she kept there. Once she had been forced to hide her magical things from her parents so they wouldn't discover them, but now she had no such fears.

She opened the bag and took out some small red candles. These she arranged in a circle on her bedroom floor. In the center of her circle she placed a small incense burner and the statue of the Goddess that sat on her altar. Then she turned off the lights so that the room was shrouded in darkness, with only the light of the waning moon to illuminate things.

Returning to the circle, Kate sat cross-legged in the center, her hands clasped gently in her lap. She remained like that for a few minutes, quietly breathing in and out and focusing her thoughts. She pictured all of the small doubts and worries that cluttered her mind being blown out when she exhaled, scattered like leaves in the wind. When she breathed in, she imagined herself breathing in light and warmth.

When she felt ready, she began lighting the candles one at a time. As the ring of fire grew around her, she pictured it glowing with golden light, making a circle of protection in which she could safely rest and do her magic. As she lit each candle she silently cast the circle by saying to herself, *With each flame my circle grows stronger*. When she had lit the last one she sat up straight, pictured in her mind a circle of fire whose walls rose up around her, and said aloud, "My circle is cast."

Now she turned her attention to the incense. She held a match to the cone that sat in the center of the burner and watched the cone begin to glow and smoke. She extinguished the match and sat back, closing her eyes and breathing in the scent of amber, cedar, and patchouli. Smelling the sweet, earthy scent made her feel as if she were in an ancient temple somewhere, a temple dedicated to the goddess Isis, or perhaps Cerridwen. It didn't matter what name she used—they were all names for the Goddess, and Kate knew that she answered to many different names.

Kate opened her eyes and looked at the statue

in front of her. It represented the goddess Demeter, the Greek earth goddess. Demeter's face wore a serene expression, her lips turned up in a gentle smile and her eyes looking out at Kate with a motherly expression. Looking at the statue, Kate felt a sense of acceptance and love. It was the same feeling she felt when she was in the midst of her friends in a circle, or during a ritual.

"Thank you for sending me on my journey," Kate said, addressing her remarks to Demeter but actually speaking to the Goddess. "Thank you for the challenges, and for the help you gave me during the year. It wasn't always very easy, but it was definitely worth it."

She thought about everything that had happened since she'd first picked up the spell book the previous February. During that first ritual she'd done, she hadn't been concerned with learning anything about Wicca, or with becoming a better person. She had only cared about getting what she wanted, getting Scott Coogan to fall in love with her. As she'd done the Come to Me Love Spell, she hadn't thought about the consequences of her actions or about how her selfish act might affect other people. She had wanted to use magic to get something for herself, not to help anyone. She'd had no interest in knowing what witchcraft was *really* about. She'd only been thinking of herself.

Things had certainly changed since that night, particularly when it came to Kate's relationship with people. Scott had come and gone, as had her romance with Tyler. She and her family had learned a lot about each other. She had lost friendships with Sherrie, Tara, and Jessica, only to later reconnect with Jessica and Tara in a new, better way. Their friendship was stronger now than it had been before, and Kate was glad that the two of them were considering taking the Wicca study class when it started up again. As for Sherrie, well, Sherrie was always going to be Sherrie. Kate had to laugh as she thought about the run-ins she, Annie, and Cooper had had with her former best friend, from the infamous slapping incident between Sherrie and Annie to Kate's own mud-wrestling encounter with her on the floor of the school science lab. *They say that in Wicca every challenge makes you stronger*, Kate thought. *If that's true, then I definitely have Sherrie to thank for making my magic muscles bigger.* She had a feeling Sherrie would give her a few more workouts in the coming months, but she knew now that she could handle anything the other girl threw her way.

The point was that now, sitting in the same room a year later, she was a wiser person. She understood that the purpose of Wicca—the *only* real purpose of Wicca—was to help each witch learn more about herself, the world, and the differences she could make in both. It wasn't about getting things, or controlling other people, or manipulating situations. It was about connecting with the energy that flowed through everything, and using that energy to create positive changes.

When Kate thought about how she'd taken the Ken doll and used it to represent Scott and make him notice her, she felt both embarrassment and gratitude. She was horrified to recall how elated she'd been at realizing she could make a guy like her, and how eager she'd been to try even more spells that she had no business doing. She wanted to forget all about that person, to pretend she didn't exist. But if it hadn't been for the girl she'd been at that point in her life, she would never have met Annie and Cooper. It was her misfired spell that had made her seek out Annie and, later, Cooper for help. It was her foolishness that had started the chain of events that would end the next day, when the three of them were going to be initiated into the same coven.

Once again she thought about the idea of cycles. Just as her relationship with Tyler was changing and becoming something else, her relationship with her friends was becoming something else. They'd gone from being three very different people forced together through fate to being three people who, while still very different from one another, had learned how beautiful and powerful those differences were. They had discovered how to take the things that made each of them unique and use those things to make magic, to make changes in their lives and in the lives of others. They had journeyed a very long way together, and while their final step was, in a way, bringing them back to where they'd started, it was bringing them back as stronger, wiser, and happier people.

And we'll just have to wait and see where the next cycle takes us, thought Kate with a sense of peace mixed with anticipation. She knew that wherever their path led them, she would be ready to face the challenges she met there.

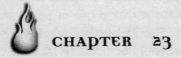 **CHAPTER 23**

"Is this what it feels like before you go onstage?" Annie asked Cooper as they waited with Kate in the guest bedroom of Archer's house. The three of them were standing, too nervous to sit, on the big wooden sleigh bed that took up most of the room.

"I think this might be worse," answered Cooper. "At least when I go onstage I know what to expect."

Kate was looking at her reflection in the mirror that hung over the dresser at the end of the bed.

"Is my hair okay?" she asked her friends.

Cooper groaned. "You look *fine*," she said.

Silence descended. The three of them had been making small talk for the half hour since Archer had led them to the room and told them to wait. There they had found three new white robes, which they had been told to put on. That's what they were wearing. The robes were loose, and there had been no belts provided for tying them, so they fluttered around the girls, making them look like ghosts.

"I feel like Casper," remarked Cooper, flapping the arms of her robe and making the other two giggle.

"I think we're supposed to be serious," said Annie reproachfully. "Isn't this supposed to be a solemn occasion?"

Cooper gave her a look. "As if we're *ever* totally solemn," she said.

"Well, we can *try*," Annie replied, feigning irritation.

"Yes ma'am," said Cooper.

They tried listening at the door to see if they could hear anything, but the bedroom was on the second floor of the old farmhouse Archer lived in, and the coven meeting was downstairs in the living room. The girls couldn't hear anything at all, which made the waiting even harder to take.

"Remember our dedication ceremony?" Kate asked, sitting on the bed. "They had us blindfolded in the storage room at the bookstore for hours."

"It wasn't hours," Cooper said.

"But it felt like it," remarked Annie. "I was so scared, especially when we had to list the gifts we were bringing to our journey."

"Do you remember yours?" Kate asked her.

Annie thought for a moment. "Honesty," she said. "Curiosity." She paused, trying to recall the third. "Oh, yeah," she said. "Patience."

Kate and Cooper gave snorts of laughter.

"What?" Annie demanded. "I'm patient."

"Then why are you tapping your foot?" Cooper

said, pointing to Annie's rapidly moving toe.

Annie stopped tapping. "Fine," she said. "What were your gifts, Miss Smarty Pants?"

Cooper sighed. "That was so long ago," she said. "I think they were creativity, loyalty, and stubbornness."

This time Annie joined Kate in laughing. Cooper didn't even bother to argue with them, knowing they were making good-natured fun of her mulish nature.

"Kate?" Annie asked when they had finished laughing.

"Willingness, friendship, and doubt," Kate said automatically.

"How do you remember so well?" Cooper asked her.

"Easy," Kate answered. "I looked in my journal last night. I write *everything* down."

"Actually, I think we did pretty well with our gifts," said Annie thoughtfully. "I know I used mine a lot."

"Same here," agreed Cooper. "Especially the stubbornness part."

"And what about our challenges?" said Kate. "Mine was truth. That certainly has come up again and again for me this past year."

"Mine was healing," Annie said. "When I think about how much I was hurting because of my parents' deaths, and how now I have you guys and a big new family, I can't think of a more accurate challenge."

"Connection," said Cooper. "That was my challenge. I didn't know what it meant then. I thought it had something to do with connecting to the natural world or something." She laughed. "Man, was I wrong. I was such a loner then, and I was so proud of it. Now I have you two in my life, plus T.J. and Jane and Sasha and everyone in the pagan community. We won't even get into how I've connected with my parents."

The three of them were quiet for a minute as they thought about how far they had come in their year of studying Wicca. Each of them had started out on the journey with some fear and hesitation. Each of them had stumbled from time to time. But now they were at the end of the path, standing together and waiting to enter the next phase of their lives.

"We did good," said Cooper, looking at her two friends.

"We did *well*," Annie said, correcting her.

Cooper was about to say something sarcastic in return when there was a knock on the door. It opened and the girls saw Robin, one of the women from Crones' Circle and one of the members of the new coven, looking in at them.

"Ready?" Robin asked.

The girls looked at each other. They all nodded without speaking.

"Come with me," said Robin.

She turned and walked away. The girls followed,

with Kate going first, followed by Annie, and then Cooper. When they entered the hall, it was filled with golden light that came from dozens of candles that had been placed along both sides of the hallway. They walked between the candles until they came to the stairway. Candles had also been placed on both sides of the stairs, forming a path of light.

Robin descended the stairs, the girls following her. At the bottom she motioned for them to stop. They could see that the path of candles continued down another hallway and stopped at the entrance to the living room, the door of which was shut. Two other coven members, also dressed in white, stood outside the door.

"You have journeyed far during your year and a day," Robin said to them. "Your destination lies beyond that door. If you are ready to enter, then proceed."

Kate, Cooper, and Annie looked at one another. This was it, the end of their journey. It was what each of them had been waiting for all year. Annie held out her hand to Kate, who took it. Then Kate held hers out to Cooper. Linked together, they walked down the hallway to the doorway.

"Welcome," said one of the robed figures, a woman the girls had never met before.

"Welcome," said the other figure, a woman the girls recognized from several of the open rituals they'd attended.

The second woman held a lit candle, and the first woman produced two bundles of sage leaves, which she lit by holding them to the candle flame. When the bundles were smoking, she handed one of the bundles to the second woman.

Working together, they moved the burning bundles of sage leaves around the girls' bodies, creating clouds of smoke. They started at their feet, moving up over their heads and then back down again, purifying them with the ritual herb. When they were finished, the two women stood on either side of the doorway. The first one knocked.

The door opened, and the girls saw that the living room, like the hallway, was filled with cheerful candlelight. The two women outside indicated with sweeps of their hands that the girls should pass through.

"Enter, and be welcome," they said as first Annie, then Kate, then Cooper walked through into the living room.

A large circle of candles had been arranged in the room, which had been emptied of all its furniture. Ringed around the circle were the members of the coven. Some of them the girls recognized, while others were unfamiliar to them. But all of them were smiling at the three initiates, and the girls felt their nervousness slip away.

There was an empty space between two of the coven members, and it was through this opening that the girls passed into the circle. When they were inside, Robin and the two guardians of the door came in and closed the circle. Kate, Cooper, and Annie were now standing in the center, surrounded by their soon-to-be coven.

Archer and Sybil, the friend with whom she'd decided to start the coven, stepped into the circle, one from either side. They came to stand together in front of the three girls.

"Tonight is a very special night," Sybil said. "Tonight we not only initiate three new witches into the Craft, but we see the birth of a new coven."

"A coven is a family," Archer said, addressing the girls. "This will be your magical family. You will share with them, learn with them, and celebrate with them. Turn now and look at the faces of your family as they speak their names."

The girls turned to look at the women and men gathered around them.

"Helen," said one of the women, beginning the naming. The girls looked at her, and saw her smiling back at them.

"Jack," said the man beside her.

And so they went around the circle, with each person giving her or his name in a clear voice. "Mary." "Crow." "Joshua." The girls listened as the names were spoken. "Pru." "Robin." Each new name brought a new face, a new smile, until they came to the final person. "Eleanore," she said, nodding shyly.

"This is our coven," Sybil said. "And we name ourselves the Circle of the Dancing Goddess."

Archer stepped forward. "And now it is time to welcome the newest members of the coven," she said. "Will you kneel?"

Annie, Cooper, and Kate knelt as instructed. Four of the coven members stepped forward from the circle and came to stand around them. Each person held something in her or his hands, although the girls could not see what the things were.

"A year and a day ago you dedicated yourselves to walking the Wiccan path," said Archer. "You followed the voice of the Goddess as she called you to come to her. That path has sometimes been difficult, and sometimes you were tempted to turn back. But you continued, moving forward and meeting each of the challenges presented to you. Now you have come to this place, this place of magic and love. Here you will receive that which you have sought for so long."

One of the coven members, Pru, stepped toward the girls. She held a small bowl of salt in her hands. "With the element of Earth I consecrate you," she said as she took a little salt and sprinkled it over the head of each girl. "May it give to you the strength of mountains."

She stepped back, replaced in front of the girls by Crow. He held in his hands a long white feather, which he swept over the heads of the three girls. "With the element of Air I consecrate you," he said. "May it give to you the inspiration of the new morning."

Next to come to them was Eleanore. She held in her hands a white candle, which she moved over the girls as they knelt in front of her. "With the element of Fire I consecrate you," she said softly. "May it give you the passion of first love."

The final coven member to appear before the girls was Jack. He sprinkled their heads with water from a silver bowl, saying, "With the element of Water I consecrate you. May it give to you the mystery of the sea."

When the four of them had finished their part of the ritual, they returned to the circle, leaving the girls with Robin and Sybil.

"Stand," Sybil told the girls.

They rose to their feet and faced her. She held in her hands three blue cords, matching the cords that bound the robes of the other coven members.

"These cords are symbols of your commitment to the coven and to the Goddess," Sybil said. "Before I place them around your waists, you must answer me a question."

She stepped in front of Annie. "Do you come here of your own free will, ready to follow the path of the Goddess wherever it may take you?"

"Yes," Annie said.

Sybil tied one of the cords around her waist before moving on to Kate. "And do you come here of your own free will, ready to follow the path of the Goddess wherever it may take you?"

"Yes," answered Kate, receiving her cord.

Sybil repeated the question a third time for Cooper, who barely waited for her to finish before saying, "You bet."

Sybil smiled while tying the cord around Cooper's waist. Then it was Archer's turn to speak. She went to Annie.

"You have been consecrated with the elements," she said. "And you have pledged yourself to the Goddess. Welcome, new-made witch."

She kissed Annie on both cheeks. She then repeated the ritual with Kate and Cooper, welcoming each of them with a kiss. When she was done she looked at them and smiled widely. "Merry meet and blessed be, witches!" she said happily.

"Merry meet and blessed be!" echoed the rest of the coven.

As the three friends looked at each other, someone began playing a drum and the coven began singing.

"Merry meet and blessed be, daughters of the Goddess!" they sang, clapping along with the drums. "Merry meet and blessed be, children of the Craft."

Cooper, Kate, and Annie looked at one another. It was over. They were witches. For a year and a day they had worked and studied, practiced and learned, and now they were members of the Circle of the Dancing Goddess. All around them their brothers and sisters of the coven were celebrating the end of their journey.

But as the three friends embraced one another and prepared for a night of celebrating, they knew that it was really only the beginning.